My Husband Wants to Keep Me Gay

Sam Wicker

Books by Sam Wicker

I’m No Hero Trilogy
I’m No Hero
I’m Your Hero (2026)
I’m His Hero (2028)

The My Husband Wants Series
My Husband Wants to Keep Me Pristine
My Husband Wants to Keep Me Dominant
My Husband Wants to Keep Me Gay
My Husband Wants to Keep Me Sated (2026)

Standalones
The Bell Earth Witch
Isekai Detective (2027)

Sam Wicker

My Husband Wants to Keep Me Gay

Book 3 of the My Husband Wants Series

Dedication

To those who prefer to laugh instead of cry, and those who need an escape.

Content Warnings

Use and mentions of drugs, drinking, mentions of necrophilia, gore, war, sexually explicit scenes, and teen sex.

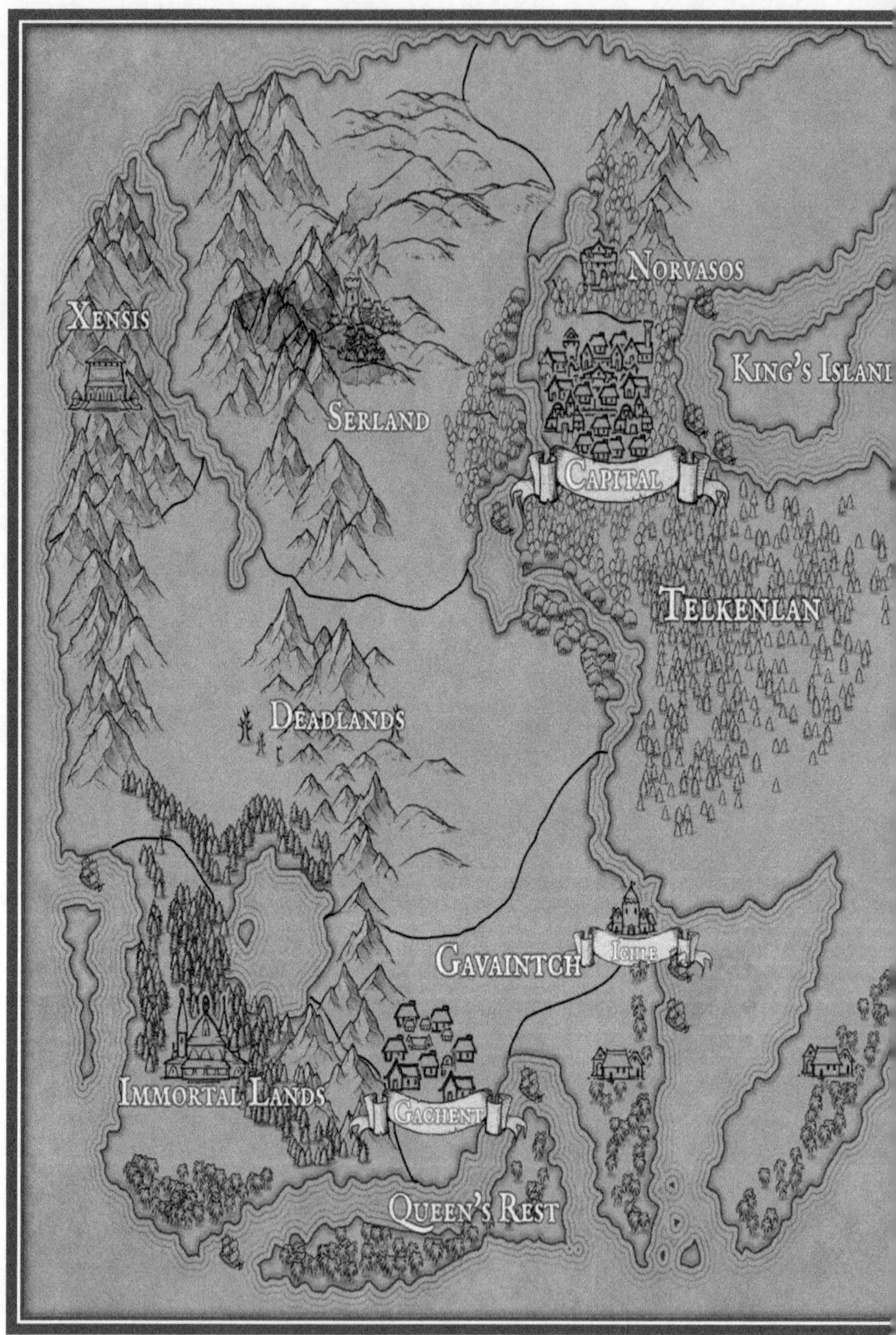
Xensis
Serland
Norvasos
King's Islan
Capital
Telkenlan
Deadlands
Gavaintch
Ichle
Immortal Lands
Gachent
Queen's Rest

Chapter 1: Oh Brother, Brother, Where Art Thou, Oh Brother

"Put that thing away! Put it! Away! Damnable! You are no brother of mine!"

"Now, Doxy," Percy crooned, "is that any way to treat me? Your most beloved eldest brother?" He ran a hand along the length of the cage he coddled. His steps were steady toward his screaming sibling.

Doxy's heart rabbited, and he thought he would burst from the inside out. His entire body shook, and a cold sweat erupted on his face. No matter how fast he moved around the drawing room, Percy became one step closer than the last time he looked. Was that thing in the cage getting bigger, too? The gods of fear needed to leave him alone.

He climbed onto the back of a plush chair, reaching for the thick drapes that hung from the large picture window. He clung to them, wrapping all his limbs around them except the one holding his weight on the back of the chair. "Stay back!"

"Come now, it's only a little bitty squirrel. It's even in a cage."

The way his brother talked to him made him feel like a toddler fighting his nap time. He narrowed his eyes, swallowing down the rabbit that tried to crawl up from his chest and into his throat. "That thing is enormous!"

Doxy gritted his teeth as Percy lifted the cage and peered into it as if the tiny crisscrossed wires weren't easily seen through. He waited for the beast inside to unleash its fury. It was nice knowing his eldest brother while it lasted.

Percy clicked his tongue, even tapping the door of the cage.

His body lurched as if the cage had opened when the thing inside chittered and the fluffy tail twitched. He wanted to be out of this room. He glanced behind his brother. The beast lay between him and the only escape. "I'll come home more often! I'll polish your boots! I'll take care of your horse! What do you want?!"

"Have Fedvich come here."

Doxy blinked and stared at his brother. Those bright green eyes didn't shift, but they held steady. "What do you want with Fedvich?"

Percy sat the cage on the small table in front of the chair where Doxy perched precariously. "I need his expertise, but I don't want to send a messenger and have word get out that I've hired him."

He swallowed hard, the fear still gripped him, but another emotion reared and overrode it. "Expertise in what, exactly? Wielding dual swords? Archery?"

"I need him as a Son of Gachent, Dox."

His brother's cheeks were flushed, and the eyes strayed, looking at the floor. "Put it away," Doxy heard his own voice come out like a frog's croak.

"Not until you promise."

"I fucking promise to get Fedvich to teach you how to fuck!" Doxy bellowed.

Percy chuckled, with a shake of his head. "I'm glad we're the only ones home and our servants don't gossip." He picked up the cage and left the room.

Doxy breathed finally. He eased himself back down into the chair, noting the wrinkles in the drapes. His mother would smack him for that later. He ran his hands through his hair. It had gotten longer, and the stuff was usually everywhere but where he wanted it. Today it was tickling his ears and falling right between his eyes to attack his nose.

Why wasn't Percival able to ask him like a normal person?

Doxy covered his face, rubbing his brows and eyes, before his cheeks to calm himself down. He was fine. Everything was well. He didn't get eaten.

What was Percy going to do with Fedvich?

It was common knowledge that the Sons of Gachent instructed in carnal delights. Did Percy have a lady he was interested in and needed to make that much of an impression?

Surely his brother wasn't the type to deflower a lady without wedding her. Was he?

Silac was somewhat. Mattias knew the composition of cum, and that was all that mattered to the academic. Doxy shuddered, trying not to picture his brothers with partners.

Fedvich kissing Percy entered his mind.

Doxy stood and paced the room. How many times did he have to tell himself there wasn't a chance of Fedvich paying him any mind? How many times did he have to tame his heart when Fedvich teased him? Maybe he should hire Fedvich.

That would be the only way to get the redhead's mouth on him.

"Dox, I wa-"

"You cannot have him." Doxy stared at Percy as Percy stared at him. What had come out of his mouth?

"I cannot have who?"

There was something in Percival's tone, the way his eyes gleamed, and the way his body was too relaxed. The eldest was up to something. Doxy was in that something and he didn't like it.

Percy's plans were never to his benefit, and always to his downfall.

"Fedvich."

"He's for hire, isn't he?" Again, Percy's usual absent-minded scratching at the patch on his thigh was too ordinary. He was trying far too hard.

"Yes. He is. I think. He might not be. No, he isn't." Doxy's words rushed out of his mouth as his brain came up with them. "He's busy."

"Busy with what? Too busy to get paid well?"

"He's busy training me!"

Percy tilted his head back. "Training you for what? Archery? Double swords? Or is it one fleshy sword?"

There it was. Doxy walked right into whatever Percy wanted. That triumphant glow on his pale face set Doxy further on edge. If he wasn't careful, his heart still might burst. Or break. "Archery." Why was it so hot in the room?

"It's about time you spent time with him. Although I had hoped for other training for you."

Doxy watched Percival's smile travel from eyes to his lips. How was it he possessed the capacity to watch over every single one of his siblings and know their every need? Doxy didn't even understand his own needs or wants. "You did all of this to get me to admit to having Fedvich train me?"

"No, I did all this to make you think about *getting* Fedvich to train you." Percy lifted a shoulder and sat down. He readjusted his pant leg with a groan, tugging the fabric so it settled better on his thigh.

Doxy pulled a small tin out of his pocket. "Harry said for you to try this." He tossed it to his brother and sat across from him.

"How is he treating our dear sister?" Percy demanded, unscrewing the tin and sniffing the balm inside. He made a face while muttering, "Why do all these things have to be so rank?"

"They don't leave the room except to forage for food."

Percival laughed. "Well, he warned us that would happen." He frowned, putting the lid back onto the tin. "I am glad that she found someone worthy, but to have the youngest married off first was not my plan."

Doxy rolled his eyes as he asked, "And what is your grand plan for all of us siblings?"

"For you to be happy, of course. I need one of you to give me an heir, for I doubt any woman would want to touch my disease."

"You don't know that." Doxy hated seeing Percy sell himself short. There was a woman out there, they just had to find her. If he had any chance with Fedvich, it might ruin him for anyone else. He imagined a future solely with Fedvich. But his brother needed an heir, too.

He glanced up, watching Percy watch him. "What?"

"I do not mean for you to give me an heir, Dox."

"What? Do you read minds now?"

"No, you were pouting and you have a one-track mind."

"Well, forgive me for not being the grand strategist, Percival Pomm. You are the one who must have your own heir.

The rest of us are too lowly in mind to have offspring to meet your standards."

"I'll take Adeline's firstborn. Half a brain from Harry is adequate."

Doxy rolled his eyes and murmured, "Yet again, I'm never going to be good as The Seven."

"Of course you will. One day. Only not today."

Chapter 2: Be a Tease, Will You, and Make Me Dream of You Again

"This is odd."

Fedvich glanced up at Charn who sat across from him. The broad man was wiping his hands on an apron before discarding it on the table. "What is odd?"

"Where are your acolytes?" Charn asked, leaning both his elbows on the table and crossing his arms.

This part of the castle, the dining room in particular, was quiet at this time of day. The sun beamed its bright rays through the tall, open windows. A light breeze carried the hint of songbirds among the trees surrounding the estate. Charn's curls stirred, unsettling from their previous raucous charm to another.

Fedvich remembered when the man's voice empowered them all, and the moment he'd all but died. Charn didn't think his life worthy without his voice. Fedvich knew otherwise.

"I wanted to spend time with the best of us." Fedvich made sure not to drip too much sex appeal into his voice. Charn was fast to leave with heavy teasing.

"Then you should have sat in the kitchen."

"I dare not. Seeing you in your element is too much for me to bear."

He kept Charn's gaze. Charn's lips twisted, and he sat back in his chair. "With Harrick balls deep and Regus gone to do the same, you're lost, aren't you?"

"I wouldn't mind letting you do-"

Charn rolled his eyes, his voice dropped from a high pitch to a harsh whisper after he swallowed. "While you may be hard pressed, I don't need sex every time I drop my pants."

Fedvich chuckled and stated, "I cannot wait for the day when you fall in love." He meant it with his entire being. The big bear across from him needed something to cradle in those arms.

"If it happens," his voice rose in pitch again, "I doubt I'll be as lucky to have someone keep me that long in bed."

His heart ached for the deep baritone, and the way Charn's voice warbled now. He was about to say something that would make the other man happy when Doxy strode in. The pup-like man walked stiffly, and his set jaw somehow made the rounded cheeks puff with his slight pout. His heart ached in an entirely different way when Doxy stood over him.

"Well, hello," Fedvich said noting how close Doxy was. He peered up at the other man.

"Hello. Hey. I-" Doxy false started several more times before he took in a deep breath, and the dispersal made his cheeks puff out more.

"Yes, he wants to eat you, so your nervousness is making him want you more." Charn said, his bright blue eyes flicking back and forth between the two.

Fedvich's grin crept out as Doxy's precious face grew red. "I hardly want him any more than I always have."

Doxy squeezed his eyes shut as his hands fisted at his sides. "My brother, Percival, wishes to purchase your... services." That last word was ground out between his teeth.

"Oh?" He hoped Percy was purchasing his services for his little brother and not for himself.

"I told him you were busy. So busy. But I think he might need you. Cause you make others feel better about themselves. And Percy needs that. He, in fact, does. And if you are acquainted with any ladies who wouldn't mind... mind a... few physical flaws. Not that he can't perform. He just has this thing that we don't like to talk about-"

"Give him a second and he will tell you everything he remembers from childhood to now." Charn whispered, leaning across the table toward Fedvich and propping his chin up on his palm.

"-but it might turn off some ladies or be rather difficult to find pleasure with that certain flaw rubbing the way it would. If you know anyone and you might introduce them, that would be grand and something that I would prefer you to do instead of fuck my brother."

Fedvich stared at Doxy, expecting the rambling to go on once the man caught his breath. He glanced at Charn and saw the same gleam in his eyes. Fedvich turned his attention back to his desire to ask, "Does your brother prefer me to be more feminine or as I am?"

Doxy's face turned a darker shade of red as his eyes widened. "I don't know that! I think he would like you as you are because as you are is perfect and you're very aware of that. Everyone knows it. Percy has made comments here and there about some women and men that we've met and seen, but he's never dated, not that I recall. He has this calmness about him; I think several people mistake for indifference or something, or that's what our mother thinks. I heard her talking to Father about us one day. But I'm going to get to the point. If you think that there is another Son of Gachent nearby that's as good or as pretty as you are and would treat Percy well, please let my brother hire him instead. I think that would be much better for me. For Percy. Percy is the important one here. Not me. I didn't say that. I have said nothing. Disregard everything!"

Charn was making the table shake with silent laughter, and it proved to maximize the difficulty of keeping his own amusement locked away. There was another emotion he was wrestling with as well. Hope. Doxy didn't want him to touch Percival. Why? Was Doxy jealous? Or did he think it would be embarrassing for him to see the issue Percy had? Or did Doxy feel as though it would grow an awkwardness between them?

Please, for all the gods and their mercy, let it be jealousy.

He took too long to say something.

"Please?" Doxy pleaded with his eyes. "Do you think you can do that?"

"Do what, exactly? Serve your brother? Find someone else to serve your brother? Or forget this entire conversation and do something else that you're thinking of?"

"All of it! Except serve him!"

Fedvich shot a glare at Charn as his laughter was turning into sounds. He then stood, leaning over Doxy as the other man took a step back. His fingertips pressed against the smooth surface of the table on either side of Doxy's narrow hips, boxing him in. He leaned in close, tilting his head. He had the ability to kiss Doxy with a simple dip of his chin. "And what is that something else *you* want me to do?"

"Um... Ah... I-" Doxy stammered, his dark eyes darting from Fedvich's forehead, lips, chin, to eyes, to repeat the pattern.

"Shall I help you with some words again?" Fedvich dropped his voice to the one that made his partner's toes curl as he said, "I want you, Fedvich, to sate my every need from this night forward."

Doxy's breathy laugh feathered over his neck.

"Or do you want to say... Take me now?"

Again, Doxy laughed while getting redder in the face and fidgeting all over.

Fedvich grunted when Doxy shouldered him out of the way. He steadied himself, watching the man back away, all the while stumbling over half words, sweating, and moving his hands about as if he were trying to mold the air into something to stick between the two of them. He shook his head when Doxy bolted out of the door.

"I'm with you. I can't tell if he's just awkward and wants you so desperately he doesn't know what to do, or if he hates you." Charn leaned back in his chair, rubbing the stubble on his chin with thick fingers. "Maybe you can jump him and see if he gets as hard as you do?"

Fedvich snorted, regarding Charn with raised eyebrows. "That's the best you can come up with?"

Charn lifted a shoulder as he admitted, "You're the expert, what do you expect from me?"

"Just fuck me already, Charnchileah."

Charn grinned and stood to mimic Doxy's shuffling escape. "I like this side of you. There's someone who is not falling on your dick and you're frustrated. Just like the rest of us."

Chapter 3: I Coulda Had a Family by Now with as Much Seed as I've Spilled Because of You

Doxy understood he was making a lot of noise, but he couldn't help it. Not today. Not after what Fedvich had just done to him. At this time of day, he was living on the edge. It would soon be time for dinner, and the house would welcome the usual men into the dining hall.

He thanked the gods he had rooms both in the barracks and in the castle, for once. Even if his rooms in the house were next to Regus' and it made him as nervous as a god with only one worshiper. Or finding it impossible to rest because of how loud his lord and lady were. He didn't need to think of that.

He moaned, picturing Fedvich leaning over him again, but this time naked. It was Fedvich's hand riding his hard cock, not his own. Fedvich's breath mingled with his to make all this noise in his bathing chamber, and the redhead moaned with him.

"Gods." Doxy pumped harder, rubbing out the tension, the explosion right under the surface. Until it wasn't, until his hips jerked as his body trembled and he released with a long, low groan.

He panted, falling back to lean against the wall. He hadn't even made it to the bath yet, but he'd at least gotten naked in time. All that occupied his thoughts was Fedvich teasing him.

What he wouldn't give to experience how Fedvich felt inside him. What he sounded like when he orgasmed. Gods, what did Fedvich's kiss taste like?

He needed to get out again. Even though he'd just gotten back earlier today, too. Eating in the same room with the sex god would be torturous. He might do something abnormal, like he always did! Or worse... force himself on Fedvich.

Doxy washed himself off and redressed. He called for his horse as he approached the front doors. He froze when he heard the dining-room door open behind and to the right of him.

"Dinner is soon, Doxy Pomm, you need to eat."

That smooth voice washed over him and, as good as, negated the release he'd accomplished in his room. He looked over his shoulder, not trusting himself at all. There he was, all lean and gorgeous with that casual, warm smile brightening his already immaculate face. "I forgot Mother wanted me for dinner."

"Oh? Then relay to your brother that I will meet him tomorrow to discuss our arrangement."

"No!" Doxy caught himself, but not before the word echoed in the foyer between them. "I mean... I will tell him." He escaped his torture and ran to his horse. He made the beast gallop out of the dusk-lit grounds and toward his former home until he had a pang of guilt. "Easy Starglow," he crooned as he reached down and patted his horse's neck, letting the beast slow down on his own.

Adeline had named his horse. She named all the horses belonging to the Pomms. That was a good thought to have. He needed to keep his mind away from Fedvich, that was all. Easy.

He watched the forest give way to farmland, then farmland to the city. He rode through the capital on the main road. The Pomm estate held two homes, one within the confines of the city, and the other was two miles outside the city proper. The city shops gave way to middle-class homes, then to farms, and then to a scattering of trees. A forest surrounded their larger home, and he was trotting through it before his thoughts betrayed him.

Fedvich would ride down this same lane tomorrow. To fuck his brother. Doxy groaned, slouching more in his saddle as Starglow plodded along.

He had to come up with a way to convince Percy not to have Fedvich. At least not first. Percy had everything first. It was time Doxy got what he wanted.

With a renewed goal, he looked up. His mother stood above the steps, smiling as she waited for him. Comfort washed over him, even as he realized he was about to get smacked for the curtains. He got off his horse at the foot of the stairs. He waited for the boy to take Starglow away before striding up to his mother.

"Just the son I wanted to see." She said, keeping her grin as she reached for him.

He took his mother's hand in his. "I admit that I damaged the curtains. I'm sorry."

The Viscountess paused, her head tilting to the left and back. "What about which curtains?"

Was he incapable of doing anything correctly today? He swallowed, watching his mother's eyes narrow. "It's Percy's fault!"

Her lips pursed as she sighed through her nose. "If it is your brother's fault, why did you apologize without prodding?"

She had him there. He tried another tactic, stammering a series of random ideas as they came to his mind. It was a long while before his mother held up a hand to shush him.

She tugged him along behind her, gliding inside and leading him to the very drawing room said curtains were. Once she opened the door for them and swept in, her gaze shot to the crumpled drapes. "Oh, those curtains."

"Yes, ma'am." Doxy stood in the doorway and waited for the fan to be pulled out of thin air and land on his cheek.

When it didn't, he looked up and met his mother's gaze.

"Since you have already apologized, I suppose I shouldn't punish you." She motioned for him to enter as she said thinly, "Sit, son."

"Yes, Mother." He rushed in, sitting across from her favorite elegant chair. He sat up straight and placed his hands flat on his thighs, as his mother had taught him.

"Percival tells me you are in love."

Doxy blinked. He blinked again to make her words make sense. Where had Percy gotten the balls to tell their mother that? Was he in love?

The gods mocked him.

If Percy believed it to be true, it must be.

"Care to tell me about your interest?"

He met his mother's dark gaze and swallowed to make the fluttering and rolling sensation in his stomach and chest stop. "I uh... what exactly did Percy say?"

"That I should ask you." The Viscountess parried, the corners of her lips curling.

"Right. Of course, he said that. You two are always in each other's pockets." Doxy stood, sat back down, then stood again. He took a step away, only to return to his seat. He had to do something. Whatever was running around inside him was going to swallow him whole.

"Doxy, my little pup, take a breath." His mother's voice was soft, and her touch gentle when she took his hand.

He did as he was told, but couldn't bring himself to meet her gaze. If he looked at his mother, she would read everything off his face and already know his secrets. Down to the very last freckle. Not that he had freckles. Did Fedvich?

"Mother, I realize you want a certain... partner for me."

"I want you to be happy!" The Viscountess interrupted before adding calmly, "That is all I want for all my sons. And Addy."

She always added Adeline in as an afterthought. It wasn't out of malice, it was just Addy was one of her boys, too, at times. Then again, Addy got into more trouble than any of the others since she was supposed to be a lady.

Doxy made himself focus on the task at hand. "It will come to nothing. It's all desperately one-sided, from me to him. Him. He. He's a he."

When his mother said nothing, he spilled more words out. "You see, he's this creature that is too gorgeous and perfect and kind, and he speaks, and I get ha- he has a very pers- pleasant voice." His face was going to set the entire house on fire if he didn't get control of it. He caught the smirk his mother tried to hide behind her floral teacup. That was a good sign, right?

"Does this voice tame beasts or incite them, I wonder..."

Doxy whimpered, dropping to the seat beside his mother and covering his face with his hands. "Mother, I cannot do this. I am completely taken with him and I'm not even noticed!"

"Now I doubt that, tell me of your last encounter with him and let's see."

He ran through the episode in the dining room of his latest failure in his mind. Doxy refused to uncover his face because he was sure he was on fire. His mother didn't need to see her own son melting.

"Given your mortification and how you have such hesitation in telling me about it, I'm sure you were noticed, my love." She said over the swish of her skirts.

Doxy sensed the cushion of the little double seat shift beside him, and her delicate fingers gently tugged his hands away from his face. He stared into eyes that were a shade darker than his before dropping his forehead to her shoulder. "Ma, tell me what to do."

"You've got to tell me how he is around you first. Otherwise, I may give you the wrong advice." His mother held his hands in her lap with one hand, while the other ran through his disheveled hair.

"No need, I've invited him to dinner tomorrow night."

Doxy whirled and stood, tumbling his mother from her seat. He pointed a finger at his brother. "You! You! *You!*"

"Careful, little brother, I might think you are worshipping me."

"Percival!"

Doxy blinked and looked down at their mother. "I'm sorry, please forgive me. I didn't mean to..." he stopped when she held up a hand and smoothed her skirts. When his brother snorted though, he returned to brandishing his best weapon. The pointing finger. "You tell him there was a mistake! Uninvite him!"

"Now that's rude, Doxy! I didn't raise you to be that way." His mother glared past him to Percival when his brother said the same thing. "Who raised whom, dearest?"

A small spark of triumph flickered when Percival sheepishly rubbed the back of his neck, before it all faded to panic at his mother's next words.

"I cannot wait to meet this man who has flustered you so, dear Doxy."

Chapter 4: If I Don't Know, I'm Innocent, Right?

"I wish you had at least *tried* to flirt with me once. Hearing everyone talk about your prowess with looks and words makes me want to witness it." Adeline's remark was complete with her toying with Harry's fingers in the lap of her skirt.

"And ruin what little chance I have of capturing Doxy? Little Pomm, you are adorable, but I have my priorities." He smirked when Harry looked across the carriage at him. "Besides, Harrick Tearney knows my seductions well enough he can show you himself."

Adeline looked between the two men; her eyes widened when they stopped on her husband's countenance. "Oh! Is it when you do that thing with your voice and it's like your eyes undress me?"

Harry chuckled as he answered, "Yes, Mistress, that's one of them."

"I see. The first time I came this close," she held up her thumb pressed against the first section of her index finger, "to giving up my religion to worship you. But you used it so often I was reduced to jealousy and desperate need."

Fedvich tilted his head as he chided, "I taught you not to use the tricks too often on one person."

"I was desperate!" Harry cried while tugging open his collar, which was quickly redone by his wife.

"Obviously. Whining and rubbing one out onto your sheets every night." He needed to take Harry to a tailor's shop. It was ridiculous that his most famous student and friend was wearing an old dress uniform and owned only a single suit.

"Desperation is quite adorable on him, is it not?" Addy asked with a sly grin.

"It is and I'm pleased I don't have to teach you how to make him do that." Fedvich chuckled when Harry rolled his eyes up to the ceiling. He switched to peering at Addy. "Tell you what, Little Pomm, you can see me in action tonight."

"Are you sure you won't end up standing and drooling while staring at Doxy?"

Fedvich kicked Harry's shin. "I do not drool."

Harry grunted, and rubbed his shin with a grin. "Are you sure?"

"Have you truly ever seen me drool?"

"That one time, at the camp, with the fire..."

"All our camps had fires!"

"Should we see if Charn and Bertran need to meet a Pomm? At this rate my whole family will be taken in by The Seven." Adeline pondered over the two bickering men.

"Doxy is mine," shot out of his mouth before he thought.

After a long pause where the couple shared small smiles, Addy said, "He has it nearly as bad as you did, Sir Red."

"That he does. Hence while I bet ten whiplashes, he drools tonight."

Fedvich groaned and shook his head. "Don't bring my lack of a love life into your kink, *Sir Red*."

"We're here." Adeline announced as the carriage leaned with the turn into the front of the house.

"Be your charming self, and you will be fine." Harry reassured Fedvich as the carriage lurched to a stop.

"Don't think the Pomms go for Tearney and Gachent orgies, Harry," Fedvich replied dryly around a flutter of his heart. Oh, what in fucking gods was this sensation? His hands shook, he was sweating, and his heart... nervous. He hadn't been nervous in decades!

"Fine. A watered-down version of yourself. More than damp, but not soaked."

With Harry's grin in his face, Fedvich chuckled. "Not that your statement can be taken however I want it." He pushed

Harry toward the door as a servant opened it. He raised his brows at Addy as she gave him a curt nod. "No advice?"

"Well, you are here at the request of Percy, so... have fun?"

Once Harry had escaped and held his hand out for Addy, Fedvich held her other hand, steadying her in the narrow carriage with her wide skirts. When she stepped off, he followed the couple up the stairs and into the house. He was unable to avoid gazing at the crescent of Pomms that welcomed them.

Viscount Pomm was a stoic study, while his wife oozed a welcoming charm with a grand smile aimed straight at him. He returned in kind, bowing his head to the two eldest Pomms. When Adeline made the introductions, he gave nods to Percival and Mattais, but winked at Doxy when Adeline skipped him.

"Thank you for welcoming me into your lovely home. I sent a gift ahead of us, did you receive it?"

"We did, but you shouldn't have," the Viscountess said taking his arm after sweeping forward to meet him. "It's a perfect wine for what we will have tonight, too."

"It's too expensive!" Doxy's words burst forth. His eyes widened, and he took a step back to be behind Percy and Mattais.

"Nonsense. I shall spend the world for a Pomm." Fedvich dropped his voice, keeping his gaze nestled between Percy and Doxy so both would wonder who he was observing. Not that it mattered to Doxy, as his brows drew low and his lips moved as if pondering Fedvich's every word.

"For just one Pomm?" Percival asked with a sly twist of his lips.

Fedvich chuckled before saying, "You are the one who sent the invitation."

"Let's dine first. You and my son may talk business later." The Viscountess said, squeezing his arm and motioning for her family to lead the way.

Fedvich held still, as the lady of the house didn't move with them right away. He glanced down and imagined the calculations through her eyes. Which one was she thinking he was for, though?

"All I ask of you is that you do not hurt him. He has a tender heart hidden behind all that fluster and chest-puffing."

Fedvich placed a hand over hers on his arm. "I wouldn't dream of harming a Pomm." When she looked up at him, he gave her one of his most genuine, gentle smiles.

"I shall have to tell you this, too." Her countenance turned predatory as she said, "Have your fun. I want to see how red he can become."

Fedvich snorted, then turned his head to laugh. When she took a step, he gently held back until she looked at him again. "Viscountess, I shall ask to have one of your precious children soon, if he turns his affections to me. May I have your blessing to pursue?"

"I had hoped you were already in pursuit!" The Viscountess Pomm admitted.

Fedvich was unable to suppress his chuckle. "Oh, I have, but I shall double my endeavors if you will allow it."

"I'll allow it. And don't worry about my husband, he does as I say."

Fedvich walked with her into the dining room. He took the empty seat beside Percival, directly across from Doxy. The chatter as the first course was served provided a measure of the power dynamic. He noted the Viscount preferred to observe than participate in conversation. The Viscountess and Adeline controlled the topics discussed. He turned to the man beside him. "I thank you for the invitation, but I'm uncertain what I did to deserve the honor, Percival."

"It's Percy. Let's just say you pique my interest in more ways than most."

"That's interesting, I've had a fascination with Pomms for quite some time. I'm pleased I attracted your eye at last."

"Ooooh, he's unaware he does it," Addy murmured from beside Doxy.

Harry almost choked on his wine to cover up his laugh.

Doxy, on the other hand, looked like his chair was on fire; he was squirming so much.

Addy leaned toward her brother and asked, "Hey Dox, do you get looks like that a lot?"

This time Harry truly choked.

Fedvich chuckled as he spared Doxy a glance before returning his attention to Percy. "I haven't the faintest idea what they're talking about. Do you?"

Percy licked his lips before he stated, "I am committed to women, but you are making me question whether I should be."

"He's the one who taught you?" The Viscountess whispered loudly while patting Harry's back.

"Everything I know except how to breathe." Harry forced out between coughs.

Mattais paused in reading a book under the table to scan around the table. "Has he taught Doxy, too?"

Doxy whimpered out a sullen "No."

"Which can be remedied. All you must do is ask, like I did." Percy's gaze was on Doxy as if his teaching a life lesson.

"Indeed. I might do some lessons for free, depending on my desires." Fedvich, too, looked at Doxy. Percy was an intelligent sort who obviously adored toying with Doxy. The eldest Pomm was quickly becoming one of his favorite people.

Chapter 5: If You Know, You Know

Pre-Year of Bertran's Training, 27ish years ago

The cloth dropped from his face again. Fedvich stopped and straightened, stretching his back as he came up. He looked at his hands, covered in soot, dirt, and other things he tried not to focus on. His stomach was long empty, for the stench was too great for him to bear. But bear it he must.

He had hope that there was at least one survivor.

Untying the cloth, he tangled the ends in his hair when he redid the knot. He hoped it would prove useful in keeping it in place. He breathed in the musk lingering on the cloth and closed his eyes. With another breath in, his imagination pictured the enormous man it belonged to.

Fedvich opened his eyes and peered to his right. He didn't have to imagine, for the man was sorting through the rubble of the next house. The wide belt moved with the narrow hips over the ankle-length dark skirt as his master stepped over and around his latest pile to the next untouched area.

When he had his last growth spurt, would his be as long as his master's belt?

Doubtful.

Returning to the task at hand, he reviewed the mantras of Gachent. Even his boring training was better than thinking about the charred bone he had just touched. The exercises he had yet to do for the day he listed, instead of feeling the sticky ooze of something on the piece of rafter he pulled off the rest of the nearly ash skeleton. He swallowed down the bile and imagined what his first time would taste like instead.

"Fedvich."

The low voice startled him, and he turned mid-jump to face his master. "Y-yes?"

"The Grandmothers are here. We will dine with them, then move on."

Fedvich looked to the east and saw the women of their village spread out to search the rubble in their place. His lips trembled, relief flooding through him. "Shall I cook?" His voice unexpectedly broke with each word, surprising him.

"No. Keep me company by the fire."

The large hand that grabbed his was warmer than normal. He allowed himself to be pulled into the wide chest. He wrapped around his master and adjusted while being lifted off his feet as if he were a feather. Fedvich realized he was much smaller than the master, but he was not small for a boy his age. Man, his age. He'd come of age two years ago. Or was it three now? Time during such destruction was not measured or witnessed the same as normal years.

He pressed his face against the thick neck and closed his eyes.

"We are trained for many things. This... we are not prepared for. I am sorry this has come in your era, my young student." There was a long pause as his master walked, the movement rocking him in a soothing way. "I think there may be some good from this yet. You will recognize the comfort necessary for survivors. You will be a gentle lover and teacher to soothe the blackened hearts. Your empathy will be strong. If you allow it, Fedvich."

"Yes, Master." One of the first trainings was to adjust expectations and practices to fit each scenario. He didn't think the tyrannical rampage would be something he could or should use in his training. His master was always wise, always molding his experience to better him. If there was one thing to be thankful for in this fire-torn era, it was that he had his master.

Building a fire was unnecessary. There were plenty around. His Master settled near what used to be a fire pit, filled with rubble, and burning steadily. Fedvich helped his master take off his pack and began handing him the grate and pots for them to cook. He noted the eldest grandmother starting her own cooking nearby. Together, they would make enough for all of them.

Fedvich looked over the rubble again, swiping the back of his hand across his face. Why would the gods allow this? How could a king, who was supposed to care for his people, destroy them instead?

"Do not let the fire of rage settle within."

He jerked back, looking down at the grandmother who had appeared beside him. "Grandmother?"

"That kind of rage only destroys you, son."

He felt defeated on all fronts. His master had served this village not even a year ago. He remembered the vibrant smiles of all who lived there. The giggling children. There was not a single bad person among them. "Why them? They didn't deserve this."

"That is not a question for us to ask," his Master's voice intoned behind him.

Fedvich tightened his fingers into balls, his nails digging into his palms. "Then are we to remember their smiles in sadness for all our days?"

"Memories do not a future make." The grandmother caught his hand and pressed it flat in hers. "You give love. You give smiles. You give laughter. You give self-confidence. Those you give to will make a future with the solid foundation you have helped them build within themselves. And your training others when the time is right will allow that hope, laughter, and love to spread further. You give better memories, and do not dwell in yours."

Fedvich's chest tightened and then release with a sharp ache. "We must honor them."

"You do. You will. By living and giving."

He leaned into the weathered hand as it cupped his cheek. "I cannot be good enough to provide all that."

"You will." His master answered unbidden again. "You are well on your way to being one of the greatest of us, Fedvich. As long as you don't poison yourself with the dead and the rage of injustice."

The Grandmother continued at his side, "Allow the warriors the rage, and soothe them when they are down to boost their cause. That is what your future holds, son."

"How do you know?"

The grandmother puffed a breath, but smiled at him. "I am old. I know what I know."

Chapter 6: Flustered is the Dessert and Whipped is the Man

By the time they finished the last course, Doxy had whimpered so much that his throat was raw. The only thing keeping him from opening his mouth and speaking were the triumphant looks Percy kept giving him and the fact his father was there. So awkward. Weren't they ashamed?

"Wife, let's allow the children their playtime." The Viscount stated while standing with his dessert bowl and spoon.

The Viscountess's bottom lip protruded ever so slightly before she too took up her dish and exited after her husband with swift farewells. By the time his father and mother left, Mattais had already finished his dessert. He got up, bowed to the room, and left, too.

"I should go too." Doxy said, mostly to himself. He really should. Then Fedvich's eyes fell on him, trapping him. He struggled to catch his breath.

"This is a dangerous situation." Harry leaned back in his chair, a curl to his lips as he situated himself to watch the room with ease.

"Should we leave the three of them..."

"Gods no." Harry gave his wife an incredulous glance. "Miss this show? No."

Addy giggled, smacking Harry's arm with a shake of her head.

Fedvich reclined to see all of them as well.

It's possible you two are brothers. It's rather uncanny. You even move alike." Percy observed, pointing to the two redheads in the room. "How come you didn't fall in love with Harry first?" He asked, looking at Doxy.

"First? Harry? Why would I- that makes no sense!" Doxy laughed, hearing himself and mentally cursing the gods as he was as high-pitched as Charn. He scooped up some of the whipped cream and shoved it in. He made the mistake of looking up with the spoon still in his mouth.

Fedvich was still looking at him. Those sensual lips slightly parted and curved upward. His tongue darted out, touching the corner of his mouth with the tip, then licking his bottom lip. That bottom lip followed the tongue in before Fedvich slowly scraped the plumpness with his front teeth.

Why did he have the sensation that he'd just cum?

His eyes remained fixed on the lips as they curved upward more. They formed his name. No, he heard his name. Right? He glanced into Fedvich's eyes, and they held gazes for a second before the redhead turned his attention to Percy.

He was now lost. Devastated. What was that man doing to him?

"How is your dessert, Percy?"

How the voice basically purred his brother's name gave him goosebumps.

"It's delicious. How about yours, Doxy?"

"Flustered."

"Is it?" Fedvich asked, meeting his eyes again and leaning forward.

"Oh gods. Can I be embarrassed for him?" Addy leaned into her husband, covering her eyes with one hand but peeking through her fingers at her brothers.

"You wanted to watch him work, so you've got to be quiet." Harry hissed in her ear, then kissed her temple as he wrapped his arm around her.

Doxy felt the usual protectiveness rear up as Harry pawed at his sister.

"Fedvich? May we discuss why I brought you here?"

Percy's question drew his attention back to the duo across the table from him. His heart stopped, and time slowed as Fedvich's hand rested on the back of Percy's chair, and he leaned toward him. The gods were unfair. He should go.

"Of course! Your desire is my command, Sir Pomm."

Percy's smile differed from his usual ones. What did that mean? What was Percy thinking? Why was he- oh gods. Oh gods, no! Percy's fingers were holding Fedvich's chin! They were looking at one another. So close! Why were they so close?! Why was Percy touching what was his?!

They were getting closer.

And closer!

He opened his mouth to scream, but Percy turned his head at the last moment. What? What just happened?

Fedvich's eyes closed, a softness entering his face as he turned from sex god to listener before Doxy's very eyes.

His heart was unable to endure this.

He was going to collapse and never rise again. They would mark his stone with: Here lies Doxy Pomm, a man who never took what he wanted and died alone with a rabbit for a heart. He sat back in his chair, trying to regulate his breathing and get his face to stop burning.

Dessert! It was nice and cool. He sat back up, digging into the whip and ice cream with gusto. Wait, what had he said about dessert?

"I like you more and more, Percy."

Fedvich's tone made Doxy's mind empty, and an image of Fedvich licking his lips like before entered.

"I'm not sure I should grant your wish with your sister present, though."

"Oh, I'll be fine. Right, dear?" Addy waved a hand dismissively.

Please say no, Harry, dammit, Doxy thought to himself, not able to take his eyes from his dessert.

"Yes, Mistress. If not, I can carry you out easily enough."

Gods, he was lost. He jerked his head up as a chair scraped back.

Fedvich got up and glanced around. "Are we sure this is the place to be?"

"Let's retire to the drawing-room. "I'll inform the staff not to bother us," Percy replied, rising from his seat.

Doxy watched as the four filed out of the room. He needn't move. Whatever his brother wanted from Fedvich was none of his business.

"Dox, I'll need your assistance." Fedvich said as he popped his head back into the room.

He groaned, failing to hold himself upright any longer. He hit the bowl, and the cool cream covered his face. He sat back up, taking his napkin and wiping off as he got up to follow. Whatever it was, he'd do a fine job. The best job.

Once he crossed the hall and entered, Fedvich motioned to a spot beside him. The other three sat down. He strode to the spot, trying his best not to conjure up something wild in his imagination. Whatever it was, he was certain he would not be happy.

"Are you well, Dox?" Fedvich asked and touched his face. He touched his face! Doxy froze. Then he watched as time slowed yet again. Fedvich leaned in, trapping his chin between thumb and forefinger, and kept coming. His breath was warm along his jaw. Then he experienced a warmth press just beside his earlobe, and watched as Fedvich pulled away, a dot of cream on his tongue that quickly disappeared into his mouth.

He should pass out. He'd swooned once before. Doxy squeezed his eyes shut, willing himself to go blank. To sleep. Something.

"Dox?"

"I'm whipped." He hissed, realized what he said, and blinked into the bronzed gaze. "I-I mean I'm fine."

"Yes, you are," Fedvich crooned with a gentle smile. "Now, be a good boy and hold my clothes."

"Sure." *Wait. What?*

Chapter 7: Stripping Time with Fedvich

He wasn't sure if he preferred Doxy this way or the spluttering mess of red-faced panic. He returned his attention to the task at hand. "Percy's request is simple, and I shall demonstrate. There is something every man should do for his mate often." Fedvich took the clear, crystal-topped pin out of his necktie. He held it between his teeth. Taking the half of his tresses that were still down, up to the ribbon, he slid the pin in and twisted the mess again until it held. He untied the silk red cravat, and since Doxy's hands weren't ready to welcome the garment, he draped it over the other man's shoulder.

"There are times where you want to make a show of it, but mostly, your everyday undressing should be enticing. Simple. Little flourishes here and there. But it's the eye contact that makes it worthwhile." As he unbuttoned his jacket, he reached out with his free hand and tilted Doxy's chin up so the man was looking him in the eye. He held his finger under his chin, holding him captive until the last button slipped from its hold.

He dragged his jacket off his shoulders and arms, to catch the collar in one hand and bring it around to his front. "Doxy?"

The man didn't move. Still staring into his eyes with a blank expression. Was it blank, though? Doxy was still a terrible read for him. He stepped into Doxy's space to grab his wrists and bring them up. "You do this all the time with Regus, don't you?"

When Doxy nodded with a long swallow, Fedvich's jealousy made him clench his teeth. He laid his jacket over

Doxy's hands as he stepped back. He turned and raked his gaze across the rest of the room. Percy gave him an encouraging nod, but it was Addy's eyes he stopped on.

Bright and curious, the eyes he wished Doxy to have at the very least.

His fingers made steady work of unbuttoning his waistcoat.

He turned to Harry, and he gathered that the brightness of Addy's eyes paled compared to the lust in his lover. His favorite and best student still wanted him. That soothed some of the ragged edges Doxy's indifference caused. If only he could get Doxy to cast his gaze upon him in that way. To want him like that. To need him as Harrick used to before he'd found his goddess.

He'd make the world over again with war if it meant Doxy would need him.

He was turning into a lovesick monster.

Fedvich shrugged out of his waistcoat and dropped it on top of his jacket while he took Doxy's gaze again. "Boots are the drollest item you can take off. Be quick about it. You can only make a show with boots if you mean to keep them on, and ladies have the advantage of that more than we do." He sat and tugged his boots off with a slight grunt. "It helps if you have tight pants on so you can showcase a hard-on."

Percy chuckled with amusement. "Noted."

"I can't do this."

He set his boots side by side next to the chair he was in. He looked up at Doxy's words. His heart dropped. The man was shaking and looking down at his discarded clothes. He stood; something in him snapped as he grabbed Doxy's chin. He made the man look at him. "Regus does this all the time in front of you and I don't hear a single complaint. Do you only like other big men?"

The room fell away as Doxy's eyes widened. What he wouldn't give to just take him right there. The spluttering and half-words began, and Fedvich did his best to piece together what the other man meant.

"N-no. Y-yes. I- if there is a man I lo-lo-like it's not Regus. He could break me in half! The rest of you are so wary of him, I know I don't have a chance! Do you realize how many times he's nearly killed me and he was asleep! Sleeping! I co-couldn't possibly ever lie with him like I could yo- um... who I might love. Like!"

"It's fascinating how much a shallow brain can make so many words just pour forth like a waterfall."

"Percy!" Addy cried, reaching over to smack her brother's arm. "Doxy has a lot of thoughts. They just circle one another."

Harry had the decency not to add to the insults, but his shoulders shook with suppressed laughter.

Fedvich watched red enter the rounded face in waves and sighed. "Don't pay any attention to them. I'm the only one you need." The whimper from Doxy had him trying to figure out what that meant. Embarrassed? Needy? What? "Aren't I?"

"Gods." Doxy said the word like a curse. He gently laid Fedvich's clothes across the back of a chair before bolting from the room.

Fedvich closed his eyes, trying to find why the pain made the world spin out from under him. He crouched, then sat on the floor. He curled up on himself. The stone in his chest burdened him too much.

Warmth enveloped him as limbs prodded themselves into the holes he had left open. The familiar scent of his Harrick filled his nose, and he let the tension release. They were so tangled he wasn't sure if he was sitting in Harry's lap or it was the other way around. He looked up, seeing that the other two had left. He met the dark eyes and asked, "What did I do wrong that time?"

"Nothing." Harry tugged the pin free before the ribbon. He dropped the two to the floor and raked both of his hands through Fedvich's loose hair before cupping the back of his neck and folding his fingers together. "You can't break now."

His jaws tightened even as he pressed his forehead to Harry's. "Doxy doesn't want me." When Harry snorted, he raised his eyebrows. "What?"

"There isn't a person in this world that doesn't want you, Vich." He growled low when Fedvich started to argue. "Don't. You know it's true. Doxy wants you, he's just... shy."

"Shy? I've had shy before and it took nothing like him. This is indifference. This might even be hatred."

"He doesn't hate you. If he did, he wouldn't be around you. Remember what he said about that kid, Gem, who joined? How he hated him cause Doxy saw him torturing some horses one time? Dox avoided him. And when they were forced to train together, Doxy went out of his way to make Gem's life miserable until he quit. Right?" When Fedvich didn't answer, Harry pressed again. "Right?"

"Right."

The redheads stayed in silence together until Harry added, "Perhaps he's intimidated."

Fedvich tilted his head. "I've done everything I could to get him to relax."

"Sure. Down to twisting your own words around so they have three meanings."

"It works. Usually."

"Usually is not Doxy, Vich." Harry murmured, "Gods, he goes from embarrassed to bolting in five seconds flat, doesn't he? What happens when you chase him?"

"I haven't."

"Gods of fucking, why not?!"

Fedvich groaned, leaning his head back against Harry's hands. "I don't know." With Harry chuckling, he sighed and shook his head at himself. "There are times I wonder if I'm not fifteen again."

"At fifteen you went after what you wanted harder than you do now. Gods, you were... desire walking. Still are." Harry pulled Fedvich back, resting their foreheads together. "You were always after what you couldn't get, though."

Fedvich chuckled wryly. "I've always gotten what I wanted, eventually. I don't know what to do with myself when I don't."

"You're forgetting someone." Harry's voice cracked with the name, "Rylah."

Fedvich watched the warring emotions cross Harry's face. He did what he always did when Harry drew upon the past. "Where is our baby girl? Are you going to bring her here soon?"

He'd only seen the girl from afar these past two decades, keeping watch while Harry visited her. Lilyanna had grown into Rylah's shadow and surpassed it. Stubborn, spoiled, and yet lovable. It was true that Rylah was the only one he had wanted and not gotten.

The woman had nearly castrated him for trying.

"Still waiting for our house to finish. I'm not about to let Lily gain any of Virsin's bad habits."

Fedvich chuckled, realizing that they had distracted each other. "I will still instruct her on everything necessary."

"Fuck no! Yo-"

Fedvich stopped Harry's wide-eyed denial with a kiss.

"Gods, Doxy doesn't understand what he's missing." Harry said with a hint of a grin. "There he is. Welcome back, my Fedvich."

Chapter 8: He Knows You Know That He Knows

The cool night air hit his face and swelled his lungs. Doxy looked up at the starry sky and cursed himself. Fedvich was probably naked and fucking his brother by now. Harry and Addy would head to her old room. His old room.

He closed his eyes, calming himself. There wasn't any use in dwelling on it. Fedvich was a grown man, able to make his own choices, and a sex god. What Doxy wanted, and what he hoped to get, had nothing to do with what Fedvich did or didn't do.

But gods, the man would get his hopes sky-high only for the reality of the situation to make him crash to the earth.

"Let me talk to him! You've done enough damage with your plan, don't you think?"

Doxy's face twitched at Addy's harsh whisper behind him. He turned slightly, watching his brother hobble down the stairs behind their sister. He loved those two. Truly, he did, but he was having a difficult time reminding himself of the fact in that particular moment. "Are you not enjoying the show?"

"The show was for you, you fool," Addy huffed, her chin jutting up. She stood toe to toe with him. "What is *wrong* with you?"

"Oh, that's a perfectly fine attack, little sister," Percy muttered with a roll of his eyes.

"You have to be blunt with him!" Addy hissed back at the eldest.

"I hate how you both treat me sometimes. Blunt, Addy, really?" Doxy was simultaneously offended and somewhat relieved. At least with Addy, he didn't have to figure out the meaning behind the meaning behind the words coming out of her mouth.

"You need to fuck Fedvich."

Both Doxy and Percy grimaced at Addy's use of words and glanced around for their mother.

"I don't think my sex life has any reason to be in your thoughts, sister." Doxy sensed his cheeks grow hot and cursed at himself.

"You found out I was a dominatrix, what's the difference?" Addy asked, something twisting her lips at the corner.

"No. No. Not thinking about that. I refuse! You're married now! It doesn't matter. Go. Be happy with the beast you married!" Doxy waved both his hands in Addy's face to shoo her away. When she didn't budge, he blew his hair out of his face, only for it to fall back into his eyes.

Doxy held up his hands, trying to stop either of them from doing whatever it was they were ganging up on him about. "Look, see, this is... this isn't... I don't need any help. I'm fine. Things are fine!"

Percy's laughter made him pause.

"Don't." Doxy warned, stepping back from his two siblings.

Addy muttered to herself, "Let's try something else." She squared her shoulders, following Doxy's retreat. "Fedvich wants you, and each time you run away like this, you crush him."

Hope swelled brazenly in his chest. He tamped it down, reminding himself that Fedvich was used to having a taste of everyone. "Fine. I'll let him have me."

He watched as both Addy and Percy glanced at one another, then they both stared at him. Pity was there. He hated that expression most of all. "What?"

"You two need to talk. Really talk. Or really fuck," Addy stated with a sharp nod.

"And don't run away." Percy added, "You running away is bringing shame to you and your family."

"Shame to our family?" Addy asked incredulously.

Percy lifted a shoulder. "Gotta say something to get him to plant his feet."

Addy shook her head. "Dox, look, rejection is... hard. Difficult. But you have got to decide whether or not you want Fedvich. Toying with him is about to break him."

"Me? Toying with him?!" Doxy laughed hard, bending over because he couldn't stand steady. What were they on? Did they know who they were talking about? Were they blind? Who was telling them all this false information? Harry? What would he get out of this?

When they didn't laugh with him, he straightened, sobering at their harsh looks. "You jest. Funny."

"No."

When both said that single word together, Doxy took another step back. Were they telling the truth? Or was it the truth they believed because of falsehoods? It had to be Harry feeding them lies about Fedvich wanting him.

It was probably obvious to someone like Harry how he desired Fedvich. He caught Harry watching him watch Fedvich several times in the past few months. What was Harry planning? Was this a game?

"He knows you want him. But he doesn't. You realize he desires you. But you don't. It's weird how both of you think one thing for a second then argue yourselves out of it." Percy tapped his finger on his chin.

Addy eyed the eldest for a moment. "Do you seriously have a way to read minds, or what?"

Percy laughed.

"Dox, just do me a favor, will you?" Addy asked, a hint of exasperation in her voice.

"What's that?" He eyed her warily, watching every movement of her face and eyes.

"Kiss him."

He snorted, the warmth spreading through his midsection and on his cheeks simultaneously. "Right."

"And do me a favor, too. Ask him to train you so you get the opportunity to kiss him."

Doxy kept his eyes moving between the two of them. It seemed unlikely they intended to trick him. Still, there was something going on. "Why do you care about this?"

Addy's hands flew wide as she yelled, "We want you to be happy!"

Chapter 9: I Yearn, I Burn, I'm Already Lost

Pre-Survival of Bertran, 2 years ago, Doxy's enlistment

He'd never seen tears in Percy's eyes. He shifted from foot to foot in front of his brother, the letter of acceptance into the Norvasos Army clutched in his hand. They had talked about this.

"I'm sorry you have to go in my stead."

Doxy stared at his older brother and shook his head. "I want to go."

Percy breathed in deep and slow through his nose, drawing himself up to his full height with it. Tears still rimmed his eyes, but his lips formed a trembling smile. "Remember your training, don't whine too much, and if you get flustered, remember to count to five."

He rolled his eyes. "I will."

"Seriously, maybe even ten."

Doxy raised his eyebrows. "I'm not *that* bad!" When Percy snorted, he sighed. "I'll work on it."

"Need help packing?"

He shook his head again as he answered, "No. I just need clothes and a few personal items that can fit in a single dresser drawer. They provide everything else."

"Wonder if you can take the stuffed cat..."

Doxy's cheeks heated. "I haven't had that cat in ages!"

Percy smirked and clicked his tongue. "Oh? That's interesting. I saw it beside your pillow the other day."

"I told you to stop going into my room!"

"And I told you I'd quit going into yours when you stopped stomping into mine." Percy pointed out with a sly grin, "Besides, I need to make sure my little brothers are keeping tidy and hygienic. You need to pack everything you don't want us finding. I believe our dear sister is to take your room when you depart." Percy patted Doxy on the shoulder before leaning in to whisper, "Whether or not the cat is real, that picture of a half-naked lady under the bed must go before mother finds it."

He choked on his own spit, and his face and neck were on fire. "I do- what?! I have nothing like that!"

"Oh, right. It wasn't your room. You have the soldiers in baths picture book." Percy pursed his lips. "I'm not sure that would be welcome in the barracks, Dox. You need to burn it."

"I- I didn't... You have got to be- Percy!"

"I am Percy and you're not even counting to three."

Doxy sucked in a breath and held it.

"Deflate those cheeks, you can't pass out like you did as a kid when you got flustered." Percy smacked Doxy's cheeks with both hands, pressing the air out of them.

With his face smushed, he glared at his eldest brother and asked, "Are you ever going to treat me like a grown man?" He sighed when Percy released him with a laugh. He had his answer.

"Why is it so hot in here?" Doxy asked himself as he pulled his collar loose. He watched the dark gaze of the most dangerous man in the world flick toward him with a frown. He redid his collar and smoothed his shirt.

A rough wooden desk stretching from one side of the room to the other had Duke Norvasos and two members of his Six, Slayth and Bertran, behind it, facing the new recruits. The legends, the awe the three men in the room induced was monumental and unreal. Nervousness, respect, and fear of the men were palpable from his side of the room.

The duke signed the last of the papers and handed them to Bertran at his side. The elder stuffed them into an envelope and sealed it with the Norvasos stamp. When Regus Norvasos stood, the ten recruits automatically grew rigid. It was as if they were holding their breath.

"Welcome to the army. As you've been told, you are to protect and serve justice as the King and I see fit. You will not give the enemy quarter, nor will you use your power and status to do evil." He hit each one of them with a dark, hard gaze. "Take your ease today, for you will wish you had never been born tomorrow."

With that dreadful promise, the three smirked as if tomorrow's work was their greatest fun.

"Follow me." Regus ordered gruffly as he moved out from behind the desk in long strides and out the rickety wooden door.

The first floor of the barracks held an open area filled with tables and benches, four rooms branched out on each side. The office the recruits were filing out of was the east side room. Regus guided them through the wide path between tables and out the front door. The bright sunlight blinded them from the dimly lit barracks. He followed the four in front as they stepped onto a stage after the duke.

Before them stretched the army of The Six, the Norvasos Army. He swore each soldier before him was twice his size and looked as lethal as a wild feline. The King's army was larger, but seemed much weaker. The men and women here commanded respect and fear by standing still.

A commotion to the right drew his attention. His breath hitched as his heart skipped a beat. Two redheads were making their way to the stage. Fighting like siblings, and bickering like a married couple, but that wasn't what had Doxy's attention. One of the men glowed, each of his movements like a dance, and his voice warmed him all over.

He straightened, looking straight ahead. He had to count. Count to what? One hundred? Otherwise, he was going to make a complete fool of himself. *One. Two.* He locked gazes with the redhead with the longer hair and mischievous grin as he stood before him. Too close.

What was he saying? That he was a child. *Three. Four. Fuck.* Then the god was before him. Doxy stirred in ways he never had before. Anger, focus on the anger. He did his best to ignore the beautiful one.

Which ones were these? He shuffled through all the stories Silac crowed through dinner and training sessions. The Six enthralled his little brother. Two redheads, yes, he remembered. One was Harrick Tearney, son of the dead tyrant, and the reason the world was free. The other was a Son of Gachent, Fedvich.

No wonder he was grace and adoration incarnate.

And completely, irrevocably, out of Doxy Pomm's reach.

Chapter 10: Can't Stop the Feeling

"Dip right hip! Circle! Doxy, what the gods' balls are you doing?" Fedvich stopped clapping the time for the men and eyed the boy he wanted to taste more than air.

"I have no idea." Doxy huffed, blowing out his rounded cheeks as he placed his hands on his narrow hips.

Fedvich thought of anything but Doxy's mouth as he counted to five in his head. "Take a break. Dox, not you, come here." Remaining seated would be optimal for this discussion. Honestly, it was the best position any time he had his eyes on Doxy since he couldn't get the man where he really wanted him. He swung his legs off the edge of the stage, watching the rest of the men leave in such a hurry that they had to be starving.

Or they realized his intense desire was beyond their capacity.

Once the men were in the kitchens or the barracks, Doxy moved toward him and stopped within arm's reach.

"What's wrong?"

Doxy's cheeks puffed out again before he answered, "Nothing."

"Your mind is elsewhere; I can tell." Fedvich pulled his leg up, rested his heel on the edge of the stage, and hoped he hid himself well enough. Doxy was dangerously gleaming, frustrated, and fucking sexy.

"Why are we learning how to dance again?"

"The boys must make money somehow. There are few jobs for us now that we've squashed the rest of the tyrant's followers." Minus a handful of Tearneys that eluded their grasp, but that was for him, Harry, and Regus to track, not anyone else. "Bertran's training puts them in good shape to make a lot of ladies drool, and the entertainment district always has coin to share for an exclusive show for their most prized patrons."

"You would know about that." Doxy looked down at the ground, scuffing his boot against the straw clumped under the stage. "I'm not pretty enough to gain coin to be any dancer. Not like you."

Fedvich felt his entire body twitch, but held back the urge to physically show Doxy just how wrong he was by pressing his heel into his own balls. Pain always calmed him down. He thanked the gods he wasn't like Harry in that regard. "You are as pretty as I am, more so in some gazes. Are you aware of how many would want to ride a baby-cheeked man built like he could break them?" What he wouldn't give to have a ride or two himself.

"None."

"There is one, at least," Fedvich shot back, then bit the inside of his cheek. Damn this man in front of him. "Several, Doxy. You learn these dance moves and they will drool over you and coin purses will open."

"I don't need that kind of money."

"Then you will have to join Bertran's training." Fedvich chuckled when Doxy paled.

"Right, I need the money."

"Try the moves again." Fedvich ordered.

"Here? With only you?"

Fedvich raised his brows as Doxy's face reddened, and he glanced around as if willing someone else to be there, or hoping no one was watching. "Are you scared to turn me on?"

Doxy stammered, "I co-could never. I'm not- yo-"

What was he doing? Torturing himself, that's what he was doing. Over the past year he had a fear that one arm was going to be more toned than the other, and here he was giving his hand more exercise tonight. He slid off the stage, standing before Doxy. "Never is too strong a word for my desire."

If he touched him, would he be able to keep himself from taking Doxy? Was he brave enough to find out? Fear lanced through him at the thought of Doxy's rejection. A true rejection with an expression of disgust on the rounded face. Rejection was something he had never experienced. But he had wanted no one this badly either.

As he calmed his thoughts, he could tell Doxy was stammering through his own. If only he could figure out what went on in Doxy Pomm's mind when it came to him. While Doxy's face was one part that made the man desirable, it also made him rather unreadable. Embarrassment, sure, that was easy to read. Other things? Not so much.

"You desire all the time. Right. I get it. I would too if everyone wanted me."

"You're desired. A lot." Fedvich's heart skipped a beat when Doxy swung those dark eyes up to his. Then it broke as Doxy snorted and laughed it off.

Perhaps this hurt the most. It was a rejection, but not at the same time. Rebuffed or brushed off was not Fedvich's favorite experience either. There weren't two of The Seven that thought themselves unworthy of love, were there?

Fedvich wasn't sure he could handle another Regus. Doxy was about as broad as the man. Thankfully, Doxy was not a god or god-like, but a dragonkin. "Are you going to follow orders or stand there laughing?"

"Forgive me." Doxy straightened and stiffly tried the dance moves.

The boy was getting worse with more training instead of better.

Fedvich stilled him by putting his hands on Doxy's hips. "You're using the wrong muscles. Undulate with these here." He brushed his fingertips over Doxy's sides and lower belly. "Be more on your toes than on your heels. Loosen your knees."

He moved behind Doxy, forming his fingers around the narrow hips and dipping toward his center. "Like this."

Doxy's gasp rang out as he lurched away. He twisted with a soft cry.

Fedvich watched as one foot didn't move, but Doxy's body did. Was he so horrid to the Pomm that he had to hurt himself trying to get away? He caught Doxy as he went down, taking on his weight and falling with him to cushion him.

The boy was not at all light, and the air whooshed out of him with the impact. When he breathed it back in, Doxy's warm honeyed scent washed over him. He held sunshine in his arms, making the darkest thoughts grow along with a portion of him too.

"I-I-Fedvich?" Doxy turned, twisting again. His face went pale.

Doxy was on top of him. Hips to hips, noses nearly touching, and the boy was as pale as a new cotton sheet. If he hadn't witnessed the leg twist, the reaction would have been a mighty blow to his already tender ego.

"Take it easy. Take your time. Is it your knee?"

Doxy nodded, his lips pressed into a thin line.

"Let me handle you." Fedvich murmured, detangling their limbs to make sure the pained knee would be cradled between his legs. "Help me turn us onto your back. To my right." He tapped Doxy's ribs with his hand before wrapping his arm around him to make sure the boy understood which side he was supposed to roll toward. "On three. One. Two. Three."

They rolled together, Fedvich ignoring the pain of having Doxy's bulk on his elbow and shoulder during the move. "There we go."

Now he was on top, his favorite position. Doxy's gasp and moan did not help his own ache. Think bad thoughts, like blood and guts. The smell of death. Anything but the sweet nectar under him. He moved away quickly. Half to keep himself from humping Doxy's hip, and the other half to check on the knee.

He placed his hand over it, noticed the heat, saw the swelling tightening the pants around the joint. Fedvich took out his knife and cut along the seam. For a dark moment he thought about cutting Doxy out of his clothes completely, but he pushed the idea away. The knee looked angry. "I'm going to touch it." He looked around, wondering where Tim was, the ever-present, self-made doctor of the Norvasos army. Always present except at this moment.

"Fucking perfect," he muttered to himself as he cupped Doxy's knee in both hands. "Easy. You'll only make it worse if you jerk around." He pressed his fingers into the tender, heated tissue. The bones barely touched, nothing ground or cracked. Sprained.

"I'll be fine," Doxy said through puffed cheeks, his dark eyes squeezed shut.

"Good. Because your thigh muscles make me want to have them between mine. Let's go to my room." Fedvich waited to see if Doxy would think about taking the bait. Or show any interest.

That red, sweating face froze. Those full lips pulled wide as a barking laugh left the mouth he wanted to plunder. Gods, why was he hesitating again?

"You must like Regus' thighs then." Doxy stated as if it were a fact.

Fedvich rolled his eyes toward the sky. Regus' thighs were massive and, like the rest of the man, could rip him apart. Well, if thighs had hands. Crush him, was more the term, like a sparrow egg. "I would advise against using our dear lord's thighs for anything other than to carry his weight and Virsin's."

He stood, brushing himself off. Fedvich crouched in front of and over Doxy, crossing his arms in front of him and holding his hands out. "Grab hold."

"I can get up."

He gritted his teeth and hid it with a fake grin as he said, "You get me up, too. But right now, if you do more damage to that knee, I'll make you like my thighs the best." Did Doxy really hate the idea of his touch so much?

Doxy finally wrapped his paws around his wrists.

"All your weight on your left leg and on me."

"You can't lift me!"

Fedvich snorted, slid his foot under the ankle of the damaged leg so Doxy didn't have a chance of putting weight on it, and pulled. He stood Doxy up with himself, shaking off the grip to sink his fingers into the thick hair and pull. He jutted his own chin, looking down into the wild eyes of his prey in his arms. "You should never doubt what I can and will do for you, Doxy Pomm."

Chapter 11: Stairway to Heaven

"What'd you do to the poor kid, Fedvich? You shouldn't hurt someone during sex."

Doxy's neck cracked as he swung his gaze toward the high-pitched voice behind him. The hair gripped tight in Fedvich's hand didn't give, and he hissed at the pull. "No Sex! Not I! He! What?" He swallowed, trying to regain some semblance of reasoning and vocabulary.

When Fedvich stepped back, releasing his hold on his hair, Doxy's heart dropped. The redhead had been so close. He shook with goosebumps all over him. Charn's scent of fresh bread and rosemary filled his nose as the man helped himself to his arm, draping it over his shoulder. Fedvich situated himself under the other.

His feet were off the ground.

No one had carried him since he was a child.

The men knocked into him with grunts and a rather colorful curse.

Fedvich said with a huff, "Right, then left."

"Right." Charn nodded.

"No, it's left!"

Doxy looked down at the men's feet to either side of him. "My right?"

"We all have the same right!" Fedvich cried, running his free hand over his face. "Just stop. Stop!" Fedvich glared past Doxy's face to a widely grinning Charn two steps ahead, pulling him and Doxy along.

"Right." Fedvich stated, like he was Harry giving orders. "Left." An order, and Charn hummed a little to himself, but stayed in stride. Without another hiccup, they reached the barracks and stopped at the bottom of the narrow, wooden staircase and the three sharp turns. Half of the banisters were missing, and there were four steps missing, too.

“Who was supposed to fix these?” Fedvich asked.

Charn lifted a shoulder, jostling both of the other men.

Doxy swallowed, nerves tingling at the idea of being carried up the precarious stairs. He alone made them creak and groan as if the entire structure would collapse under him. “How about I use the wall and the banister to get myself up?” His voice sounded as high as Charn’s in his ears.

“And fall to your death as the banister cracks? Not on my watch.” Fedvich straightened. “Charn, you first.”

“That means you’ll take on most of his weight until I can pull him.”

“And?”

“Don’t you want to have energy to pet your little mate once we get him tucked in?”

Fedvich asked, “And will I have enough energy after pulling him up all those stairs, anyway? Yes. I’m not as out of shape as you, Charn the Cook.”

The way Charn snorted had Doxy thinking it was about to become a challenge between the two. “So, hey guys, let’s just uh… try it, and see? I mean I can do it myself, but you both refuse to let me do anything by myself with this knee and I’m grateful, don’t get me wrong, but I’m not so sure those stairs are gonna take all three of us, anyway. Are you?”

“Breathe.” Charn peered into Doxy’s face.

Fedvich chuckled and shook his head. “It’s adorable when you ramble.” He pushed Charn’s face away from Doxy’s.

Charn snorted into Fedvich’s palm.

Fedvich hissed, “Gods, what’s wrong with you?” He wiped his palm off on Doxy’s shirt.

“Hey!” Doxy cried, “That’s gross!” His body lifted, and his stomach left him. His brain rolled as if it was in a ball while all he could see was Fedvich’s gleaming eyes. Then he was staring at his door, Fedvich breathing harder behind him, arms tight about his waist.

Doxy noticed Charn was left behind due to the heavy footfalls and creaking stairs below them.

Nausea churned his stomach, and a cold sweat popped out over his body. He shuddered. Fedvich pressed into him, the smooth wood of his door cool against his cheek and through his shirt. What was going on?

"Take in enough air to fill your lungs. Don't pass out on me, Dox." Fedvich's lips brushed the shell of his ear.

The shock of the redhead's body pressing him against a solid surface, those sensuous lips he dreamed about touching his bare flesh made his lungs fill completely.

"There it is. That's my good boy."

Doxy's entire body thrilled like lightning. *Good boy*. Fedvich thought he was a good boy. He grinned, closing his eyes and willing the nausea down with his next large breath in.

"Did you already fuck him?" Charn asked at the last step before joining them in the hall. "Never seen that kind of grin on him."

"I can only speed through one thing at a time, and fucking is not something I rush."

Doxy noticed something brush against his lower lip. He didn't care at the moment. Fedvich pressed good against him, his door was nice and cool, and his knee was going to kill him with pain. Nothing else mattered.

"It is a pleasant face. You think that's the expression he makes after sex?"

"Only one way to find out, Vich."

What were they talking about? Knee. Right. "It's fine. I'm fine. I need my leg cut off."

"Don't be so dramatic," Fedvich said with a chuckle.

"I'll see if I don't have any pain powders left. Tim went into the city." Charn revealed as his footsteps got farther away.

The door gave way before him. Pain shot up his knee before it threatened to buckle. But Fedvich held him steady, leaning him back against the lithe body. Could one get drunk from touch? Words? He didn't have the energy to open his eyes.

"You've got to work with me a little bit, Dox." Fedvich grunted as he shifted them both into the room. "Hold on to me, or something."

Doxy warmed with every touch as Fedvich slid around him. He lifted his arms, the hard sides against his wrists until he hugged Fedvich to him. He nuzzled the man's neck. Fedvich had a spice about his scent, something only he had, and it was strong.

"Gods of fucking, why now?" Fedvich asked with a groan.

"Why what?"

Fedvich answered, "You're being all adorable and..."

He gasped as Fedvich pushed. He fell back, his eyes flying open to peer into the serene face of the sex god among them. His bed caught him, the thick tick mattress bouncing him before letting him settle into its warmth. His mind was sluggish; his thoughts were worse. He reached for Fedvich.

He stared up into the man's metallic gaze as the red hair fell around their faces.

"No magic for you."

Doxy whimpered, utterly saddened by Fedvich's announcement. "But I want it. Magic stick."

"Aaaand with that, I'm walking back out the door," Charn chimed in, two small packets held in one hand as he shook his head just inside the threshold. "You have fun with your magic stick, Doxy-poo."

He dropped the packets on the dresser and closed the door behind him.

Doxy let the curtain of red fall back down, when had he lifted it to watch Charn? He couldn't remember. But Fedvich was so close. His face was so beautiful. He giggled as he remembered what Charn called him. "Doxy-poo."

Fedvich's hair was so soft. Was it even hair? He tugged it.

The face above him shifted from beauty to downright sexual. The full lips parted, the mesmerizing eyes fluttered, and the sound that came from Fedvich's throat made Doxy's pants grow uncomfortable.

He should take them off.

Chapter 12: Fall to Hell

Doxy was hitting too many of his buttons. He was going to lose control and be completely ashamed of taking advantage of the younger man. He heard an interesting rustling and opened his eyes in time to see Doxy flick the last button open on his pants. "Fucking gods. Fucking." Fedvich cursed and whirled away.

He held his back straight, painfully so, and clenched every muscle. Jaw, shoulders, biceps, each finger, one at a time for control. He needed resoluteness. Fedvich let his training take over as he turned his head just enough to inspect the new situation over his shoulder. Doxy Pomm, both his torture and his passion.

He was pouting.

Gods fuck him, that baby face was so soft looking and that bottom lip even trembled.

Chest, ribs, abdomen, lower back, ass clenched, and the larger muscles of his thighs came next, all the way down to him curling his toes in his boots. He held each in steady firmness. Rigid. Immobile.

He would not fuck Doxy Pomm.

But oh, he was going to make sure Doxy would intimately know every inch of him one day.

The sharp whimper behind him had him looking again. Doxy was pushing his pants down in a half-hearted way. Then he'd see a button on his shirt and begin undoing those. Then go back to his pants.

There weren't enough drugs nor distractions in this world for him to get through this.

"Pull it together, Fedvich DeLorraine Gavaintch, Son of Gachent." He imagined the grandmothers staring, their eyes boring into the back of his head, into his very soul. "Powders."

He turned, pouring water from the pitcher in the room's corner into a wooden cup beside it. Those mewls and whimpers from the bed were making him want to lick them into a greater fervor. No. He grabbed up a packet from the dresser and sat on the edge of Doxy's bed. As soon as the boy opened, Fedvich poured the painkillers mixed with sleep agents into his mouth. Then pressed the water to his lips. He watched Doxy drink it all down.

Fedvich gently undid Doxy's shirt, helping him sit up. Golden skin, fat muscles on a body naturally thick, made his mouth water. As Doxy's hands kept trying to help him out of his clothes, he took the shirt and twisted it this way and that through Doxy's palms, over and under his wrists, and back again. The man lying on the bed grew distracted by trying to untangle himself.

He kept his gaze on the rounded abs. While defined, they were also like two, almost four, pillows, large and not cut deeply. He couldn't bring himself to look further down.

He gritted his teeth, put his hands on Doxy's sides, and slid them down to hook his fingers into the waistband. And pulled. Nothing happened. He shifted his grip to where it was slightly under Doxy on each side and pulled again.

Tender, warm, soft, that curved ass held the pants on well.

"What have I ever done to deserve this misery?"

He rolled Doxy to get the pants free, and couldn't help but notice something half-hard mocking him along with every other part of the boy's body. Man. Just because Doxy was a decade or so younger did not make him a boy.

For what he saw under him was definitely *all* man.

With the pants successfully down to the thick thighs, Fedvich took a break. He held his face in his hands, imagining rotted teeth, the smell of sulfur from Serland, the toughest renewal of control he'd ever completed.

It wasn't like he could let off steam later with Harry, either.

He needed to make a deal with Adeline.

A fuck from Harry for free tools? That should work. No one looked twice at him buying leather and chains. Maybe she would agree if she could watch. That would be nice. He'd still throw in a few tools of the trade here and there, though.

"Fedvich."

His cock jumped at his name being whined. He glanced over, watching Doxy stretch like a cat in the bed. His hands were still tangled; his glorious arms taught above his head.

He needed to figure out which god he'd pissed off and make amends.

"What is it like to be licked?"

"No." Fedvich didn't recognize his own voice. His entire body was tight, and he struggled while fighting a losing battle with himself. He didn't know which side of him he wanted to win. "How long does it take those powders to work on you?"

"Medicine?" Doxy's mouth worked as his body relaxed back into the curve of the bed. "I hurt."

"Yes, my darling Pomm, but you took medicine. It should work shortly."

Doxy giggled and shook his head as he said with a lazy smile, "Medicine never works on Pomms. Gotta knock us out."

It had to be more than one god he'd angered.

He'd never knocked someone out without killing them before. How did one do that? Pull back at the last second? Were there pressure points specifically...

Fedvich was an idiot. He was aware of that. He believed it with his entire, tortured soul.

With a smile down at the beauty, he murmured, "Sleep well." He jabbed his fingers into the three points and breathed a sigh of relief as Doxy's eyes closed and his body grew limp.

Well, almost all of his body.

"I'm going to take that as not all hope is lost. He wants me. Right?" He asked himself as he pulled Doxy's pants the rest of the way off, taking special care around the inflamed knee. "Right. Who doesn't want me?"

He muttered to himself in answer, "One Doxy Pomm, that's who."

"I heard you hurt the puppy."

Fedvich took longer than he liked to connect Bertran's words to what the old man meant the next morning. He stared into those sharp blue eyes and experienced the familiar internal shudder. He swore Bertran housed death itself within that war-hardened body. A change to what he was looking at for self-preservation was needed. The back of Tim's head was interesting, just over Bertran's shoulder.

"The pup-" he shot a glare at the old man, "Doxy, twisted his knee because his agility while being stared at is not ideal."

"Stop staring at the poor child."

Fedvich sighed. "That's like asking Slayth to stop bragging about his kids."

"He does it for a while. You can, too." Bertran's gruff voice stated matter-of-fact as he ran a whetstone down the length of an axe blade.

They were finally going to fix the stairs. First, they had to cut the trees.

"For damages incurred, we shall train tomorrow."

Forget death, he'd wish for it all night. "No. No!" Bertran's grin froze everything inside him.

"Oh yes, my little whore friend."

Chapter 13: What Is Life? Baby Don't Hurt Me...

All he needed to do was cross the threshold. Safety lies beyond that very door. He just needed to get up the steps. Why were there so many steps? Why did the path take forever between the training grounds and the duke's front door?

No matter. One fucking step at a time. One more step. Another.

What was life? Another step.

There had to be another war somewhere. That was better than this hellish scape. Wasn't it?

No.

One more step. Nope, we're not falling backwards. Always move forward. Never leave your comrades exposed. There it was, forward a step. Good boy.

Five more fucking steps. Weren't there five to begin with? Had he moved?

He turned, looking back down and counting. Five. He looked up. Five. What the fuck?

He groaned, reaching down to lift one twanging thigh up to the next step, then the other. "Come on, boys, don't let me down now." Since when were his thighs boys?

Probably since everyone had a dick in a cunt and didn't want to leave it. That was sound logic. Hope sprang eternal as he crested the last step. Flat, it was flat from here on out, he could do it. Everything was within reach.

He stumbled forward as the muscles in his legs screamed in protest. He was soaked, sticky all over, and stunk. Literally smelled himself, and he was never this foul. Not Fedvich. Things *on* him smelled like the blood of his enemies, cum, the shit on the streets if he didn't sidestep it in time.

Fedvich DeLorraine Gavaintch made it inside. Heaven was nigh. He looked right, knowing the second was housed there, and cursed as his eyes went up the stairs. “Fuck this.” He allowed himself to melt to the polished stone floor. “Harry!” He bellowed because his voice was the only thing that properly worked. “Get your dick out of your wife and down here!”

The stone floor was pleasant against his sweaty skin. He could die happy here. Cooled down, not running, not listening to two hundred other men panting and not getting any pleasure from it. Yes, heaven was indeed nigh if it existed.

Where were the servants? Oh yeah, that was right. When the actual mister and mistress of the house were away, the mice played. “Harrick! Tearney!” He bellowed again.

“What do you want... Fedvich?”

He was running down the stairs, Fedvich could hear him. He missed being able to move freely, without the constraint of sore muscles and a sorer pride. How was it that the whore and the vicious got partners before he did?

The sun got to him; that was the only explanation of why his mind was wandering, skipping all over the place like a child with a basket of flowers and not a care in the world.

“What are you doing?”

At least Harry had the decency to crouch down in front of his face. What he didn’t have the decency of doing was getting dressed. Fedvich stared at the thighs before trailing his gaze up to the cock and balls displayed in a towel just for him to see.

“Hating you.” The man had the audacity to chuckle and slap him on the back. That was sore there, too. He sighed. “While you have a perfectly pleasant set, they are not for me, therefore, I don’t wish to stare at your dick and sack. Move!”

Harry grumbled but did as he was told, sitting on the floor in front of his comrade, adjusting the towel so he wasn’t flashing anyone.

“Come back. Please come back.”

“You just told me you didn’t want to see my dick and balls, and now you do?”

“I don’t want *those* to come back!” He paused and added, “Yet. I want you or Regus to get your asses back to us! You know? The men, me, the soldiers who need training and my sanity that needs keeping and I really don't want to die this young because I have so much to do."

"Like what?"

Fedvich ought to have been insulted, but he wasn't because Harry obviously had less to do with his life than he did. "Find a partner who is more than a one-night stand or... relief through dry spells."

Harry lay down, his feet pointing in the opposite direction from Fedvich's, so they faced one another upside down. "What is wrong?"

"This is weird. Why are you lying there when I don't like you that much?" Fedvich stared at Harry's features, watching his teasing soften the worried countenance. In the decades that he'd known Harry, his face had changed little. But there was still something he couldn't quite put his finger on. Love? Probably, or something as ridiculous. "What's wrong is Bertran is in charge."

"He's been in charge before-"

"Not for this long!" Fedvich's blood boiled even as he wanted to cry. "Do you realize how many miles we ran today? Do you? Are you aware of how many drill sets we had to do *while* running those miles because Bertran has this rule that no one can fall more than three paces behind everyone? Huh?"

"It can't be that bad."

Fedvich wanted to fuck the smugness off that face, but he didn't even have enough strength to do that. "You run to the capital and back and do six sets of fifty."

"To the capital?!"

Fedvich and Harry both lifted their heads enough to study the woman in a robe standing at the end of the staircase.

"Hello little Pomm." Fedvich smiled, resting his chin on the floor, then glared at her because she was the reason for his current state. In a way. "Stop seducing Harry. Or fucking him. Whatever it is you're doing, stop it. At least until Regus gets back."

Adeline's countenance turned sweet. "That's not happening anytime soon, Fedvich." As she crooned those terrible words in her beautiful voice, she made her way to him.

He was about to beg, truly beg, when she sat on his ass. Concern; that was a new emotion when a woman sat on him. His eyes slid toward Harry. Fear; that wasn't new when a woman sat on him and her man was nearby. "Oh... oh gods..." he moaned, melted, and wanted to have her babies all at once. The woman's hands were magic, smoothing the pain away from his lower back and working up.

He whimpered before words began pouring out of his mouth, and he didn't care what he said or didn't say. "Adeline, I worship you with my entire black heart. You don't deserve an ass like Harry's, you need a better one, I'll find you one. Swear it. You can have mine. Me. All of me with those hands, my dearest little Pomm. I will fucking give you everything I own. The clothes off my back, my hair, everything, just so long as you don't stop."

"She's a Tearney."

"She's better than a Tearney!"

"Boys, I'm a Pomm Tearney, you're both right."

Fedvich heard himself make the oddest sound as pain shot through his back and down his arm when she pushed a particular spot on his shoulder. "Oh Pomm, please don't hurt me like that anymore." He groaned when she stopped, "But don't stop."

"Is there a reason why all members of The Seven love pain?" Addy asked, returning to her ministrations.

"Have you met Regus?" Both men asked at the same time.

Chapter 14: Happy Endings Are Made of These

There were so many bodies lying on the ground, over the benches, and even one halfway in and halfway out of the barracks door that Doxy was unsure where to start. He did another headcount. He was missing four. Regus and Harry weren't there as they were on vacation or honeymoon. Where were the other two, and who were they?

He bit back the snort at the thought of Harry being married to his sister. He was probably doing all manner of terrible things to her. There was nothing he could do about it either.

Doxy caught Bertran coming in from the pots.

Who was missing? Had they left someone behind? Impossible, since Bertran didn't let anyone fall behind by even a pace or two.

Fedvich.

Doxy bit the inside of his cheek, ignoring all the thoughts and stirrings that thinking of that man incurred. He still needed to ask him how he got to his room in the barracks. He walked himself through the headcount he'd completed earlier and didn't remember seeing the redhead. He settled the crutch under his shoulder and hobbled over to Bertran. "Have you seen Fedvich?"

Bertran raised a brow at Doxy. After a long cold stare, he looked beside him at Slayth. The two eldest members were the only ones who had run and worked with the rest of the men and were still standing. When Slayth shrugged, Bertran shook his head. "No. He was with us when we entered the lane."

"Right." Doxy waited, sure that one of them would go looking. When neither of them even shifted in their stance, he sighed. "I'll search."

As carefully as he could, he picked his way through the bodies. He hadn't seen many battles, most were small ones after the war, but he was pretty sure this looked like the aftermath of a massacre. "At least get them some water!" He called to the two old beasts over his shoulder.

"What was that, boy? You want to run?"

Doxy paused as curses erupted, and in the far corner, one man screamed as if he were being thrown off a cliff. "No! No! No running! See, I'm going. Didn't say a thing! No, sirs!"

He nearly fell flat on his face several times; he was hobbling and swinging on his crutch so fast to get away from the horrid elders. How were they not dead? There were men half their age, no! not even a quarter of their age in Slayth's instance that weren't on their feet.

Upon arriving at the castle's entrance, Doxy surveyed the lane. Not seeing anything red, he glanced back at the house. The door was wide open, and Addy was sitting on something. Curiosity got the best of him, and he made quick work of the stairs and stared.

His newly wedded sister was sitting on a man, not her husband, and rubbing him down with her dainty hands while said man was making the obscenest noises.

She even had the audacity to turn and give him her sweetest smile. In a robe. On a man. In broad daylight with the door wide open to the world.

Not to mention the noises were causing some discomfort in his lower extremities.

"Adeline, sister, what are you doing?" When he asked, the noises continued, but at a lower tone and less frequently. Then the redhead turned and looked up at Doxy with an oddly wide grin on his face.

"I'm giving Fedvich a massage because he collapsed here. What happened to your leg?"

"Twisted knee." Doxy answered, still eyeing the grin on Fedvich's face. He turned to Harry, expecting to see murder in his eyes. "Why are you in a towel?"

Harry sighed, "Do you really want me to answer that question? Or the question why your sister is in a robe and nothing else?"

"Oh! Gods!"

The cry had Doxy lifting his crutch. He saw Addy, who was facing the other direction, rub down Fedvich's left leg. He was sure the man had just cum. Doxy hoped he hadn't, the hope made him glance back at Harry. There was murder in his eyes now. What would Regus do in this situation?

Walk away.

Doxy nodded. "Addy, nice seeing you. Harry." He turned and started through the door, only to stop when Fedvich whimpered his name. He said a silent prayer to the gods before asking, "What?"

"Take me home?"

He had that look. The one where his bottom lip trembled a bit, and his eyes were wide and hopeful. Doxy both loved and hated that expression. Sometimes Fedvich got them free things, like bread from a bakery. Other times, Fedvich pulled him into the oddest situations with it.

"Harry can take you home."

"In a towel?" Harry sat up, his brow raised.

"Go get dressed." Doxy bit out, why did he have to explain everything?

"Not happening. You take him."

"I have a bad knee!"

"Use each other as crutches!" Harry held his hands out, and grinned because he had his victory.

Doxy was suddenly weary. He watched as Addy finished with Fedvich's other leg. "Good. Can we go now?" He motioned Addy to get off.

He glared a little as Addy mouthed the word 'remember' and tapped her lips with two fingers. Not only was he walking Fedvich to the barracks, but he had to kiss him too? No pressure.

Fedvich whimpered and lay still for a moment. He sucked in a breath and pushed himself up on all fours. He stayed there for a while longer before standing up. Doxy flushed when Fedvich grabbed Addy's hands and kissed both. Then the redhead was swaying toward him, hooking his arm around his shoulders, and leaning.

He half walked, half leaned, and half carried Fedvich out the door. Both stared down the stairs before braving them. Somehow, they reached the bottom without losing their footing. But Doxy's knee was not at all pleased with the situation.

"You have a death wish." Doxy stated.

Fedvich chuckled. "Whatever makes you say that?"

He was too close. He felt Fedvich's breath on his cheek. Not daring to turn his head, Doxy answered, "Kissing and handling Addy like that in front of Harry."

"Better to do it in front of him than behind his back."

He couldn't deny that. "You are heavy."

"I will not be insulted by that." Fedvich leaned more.

Doxy leaned on his crutch, and tried pushing Fedvich to walk on his own feet. Somehow, one of his feet didn't move when it was supposed to, and the crutch didn't swing either. He turned, pulling on Fedvich for balance. Then his back hit the ground, and Fedvich landed on him.

"Well, fancy seeing you here," Fedvich drawled, propping up on his elbows as if he were at home in his bed.

"Get off."

"In a moment." Fedvich's voice had a different tone.

Doxy stared up into Fedvich's eyes, which reminded him of bronze, or a metallic golden brown with green flecks. "Why did you collapse?"

"Aren't the others in the throes of dying, too?"

He had him there. "Are you still hurting?"

"I have a different ache now."

Doxy cursed. "What hurts? Did you hit something?" He tried to raise up, but Fedvich had him properly pinned except for his hands. He placed them on Fedvich's shoulders, about to roll with him.

"I didn't hit anything, Dox," Fedvich answered.

Something in the way he said that had Doxy rethink everything from his breakfast that morning to his religion. His brain stopped at the religion part and clung to it as if it were bars to his cage, holding him back from his gods. Fedvich was always there, a constant at his side, and some things the man said had Doxy's body reacting, his mind imagining, and his mouth watering. As of this instant, he wished Fedvich would kiss him while simultaneously wishing the man would roll off him and let him breathe.

"Is there anything I can do to help?" Doxy asked, his salivating mouth suddenly dry.

"Yes. Some things, but not here."

There were those vague answers that made Doxy wonder if the man was all there, or if he himself was especially dull. "What things and where?"

That's when Fedvich shifted, and something pressed into his thigh, resembling a dagger hilt under several layers of cloth. But Fedvich wasn't wearing that many layers, nor was he. "You'll figure it out one day, I hope."

Doxy was about to ask again, but Fedvich was up, standing on his own two feet and pulling his shirt free from being tucked into his tight pants to let the hem drop to the tops of his thighs. Then the redhead bent, holding out a hand to him. He took it, grunting while Fedvich hissed as if in pain when Doxy used him to stand. "Sorry, what is it? Your back?" He steadied himself while touching Fedvich's lower back. "Did Addy sit on you too long?"

Fedvich's snort was derisive as he shrugged out of Doxy's hold. "Pomms are never still long enough to cause what I need."

Rage was a quick flash. "You really do have a death wish saying something like that to me about my sister."

Chapter 15: Mistress Coldwater Never Fails

Fedvich let Doxy stew, knowing the younger man would settle down on his own. He always did. He stepped on the head of the crutch, catching the end and twirling it idly. Doxy's body under him had caused more aftereffects than he wanted, and he hoped the other was too fussy to notice.

He'd filled out so well in the two years with them. His arrival had him pale, round, and passing out after every training session. Now Doxy looked like a boy still, with his round face, messy mop of sandy blond hair, and short stature, but that was where it ended. Muscles covered his arms, chest, and legs. Doxy's stamina had improved tenfold, as he could keep up with The Seven's kind of torture.

His desire hit him when the man first smiled that sheepish smile upon introducing himself after signing his life away to them. Noting the usual fleeting lust growing and holding on like a leech instead of releasing after a few denials and refusals. This past year, Fedvich took Doxy's presence as his preferred torture.

Regus had his self-doubts eating away at him every waking moment. Harry his whips, and lust for physical pain. Charn his waking walking nightmares, and those that woke him in the middle of the night with screams and cold sweats. Slayth, with his penchant for distance from others, because he would outlive them all. Bertran's only joy rested in making others suffer. Doxy was too inexperienced to have enough trauma to cause his vice, yet.

Fedvich counted himself blessed by the gods, if they existed, to have such a minor device causing pain. In love with a twenty or thirty-something old who had only fucked twice, and the only deep relationships were family and friends. Then there were the rest of The Seven smirking, teasing, and never aiding him in his desire. Except for making sure each night he had his fist to work out frustrations in the darkness of his room.

He hated his life. The love portion of his life in particular. Mostly because it didn't exist.

"...vich?"

Ah, he missed it. His name from Doxy's mouth again. "Yes, Pomm?"

"I'm gonna collapse if you don't give me that."

He smirked, still twirling the walnut crutch. "Don't trust me to catch you?"

"Not when you're imagining something." Doxy said with a hop toward him, the foot with his twisted knee barely touching the ground.

He was trying *not* to imagine things by reliving why he had unrequited love as his destruction of choice. As he surmised, Doxy was again calm, as if he hadn't seen his sister in a state of undress with her new kinky husband mere minutes ago. Or listened to the man of his dreams making noises he could cause if he just would. Damn naivety.

Fedvich stepped into Doxy's space, holding the crutch where his companion could easily fit it under his armpit without having to hop again. "What do you think I'm imagining?"

"Probably killing Bertran, or whatever it is you're going to fuck tonight."

He wasn't wrong on either part. "Want to help?"

Doxy laughed. "I don't want an early grave. Bertran would kill me before I even realized he was behind me."

He didn't move away when the wounded settled the tool and turned back toward the barracks. Doxy's body slid against his, and the younger one muttered an apology. Fedvich made the angle work for him, tilting his head and leaning down as he whispered close to Doxy's ear, "Not that. Tonight."

That body stilled, barely breathed, and Fedvich kept his hands to himself, because if he didn't, tonight would happen now. The ear his lips were nearly touching turned a bright shade of pink. Fedvich waited, knowing the spike of hope making his heart thud harder in his chest was going to be crushed.

"Funny." Doxy said, turning to meet his eyes. He added, "I doubt a woman would appreciate trying to avoid hurting my knee."

A kiss was within reach. All he had to do was crush Doxy to him and take it. Take all of him.

Completely ruin everything.

Fedvich hid his annoyance with a chuckle and dragged himself away with a shuffling step backward. "You don't always have to suck them off first, you know?"

He pivoted around Doxy, his muscles screaming, but he needed to get away. Get to his room and collapse on his bed and never ever depart. He listened for the shuffle tap of Doxy's walk, relieved when the man could travel on his own. He wasn't sure he could take the pain of touching him any longer.

"You don't?"

An image of Doxy on his knees in front of him made Fedvich curse himself. "No." He gave a quick reply, trying to buy himself time to picture bodies cut open, the stench of bowels and piss mixing with blood and dirt. All so he could keep his dick in his pants and not mold Doxy's tongue and mouth into his pleasures. "It's a kindness."

"Oh, that's why you and Harry told me to learn. For when I get married." Doxy nodded, keeping pace with Fedvich even though he was several steps behind. "Makes sense."

Doxy and marriage. It wasn't a thing that had to happen. He had an older brother taking the title, so Doxy was free to do what he wanted, mostly. Why didn't the little Pomm see he could fuck away his life?

"Remember when you said you'd teach me archery? Wouldn't now be a good time?"

Definitely a perfect time. He was already hard, imagining his cock in Doxy's throat, frustrated and impatient because he was in too much pain to keep control, and he'd already touched the boy too many times. What was an archery lesson?

Fedvich stopped, tilting his head to look over his shoulder with a grin. "How are you going to pay me?"

Doxy flushed. Fedvich didn't breathe. Then the flush disappeared into a confident grin as he said, "I'll make you a pie." He lifted a shoulder. "I was supposed to make you one to thank you for taking care of Addy during the hunt, but I forgot."

He could kiss Addy if he wouldn't get run through with the wrong sword from Harry. "It's a date. Go get your gear. Meet me by the pond in the creek."

Click, shuffle, Fedvich half listened, half watched Doxy enter the training grounds to cross them to the barracks. The poor boy had to step over and dodge all the bodies of their comrades. He made his way to the creek, walking down the footpath to a wide sandy beach made by a bend, Fedvich pulled his shirt up and over.

He sat with a groan, cursing the third in command as he tugged his boots off. Then he shimmied out of his pants and stood. Stretching was more painful than it was worth, so he stopped midway and walked into the water. He could be out, dried, and back in his boots and pants by the time Doxy arrived.

But what if he wasn't?

Fedvich cursed his imagination as the cold took his breath away. Waiting until the water reached his waist before ducking the rest of the way in, he closed his eyes and let the water do its work. He repeated the word 'relax' mentally, letting out a bubble between his lips with each pause. He straightened, pushing his hair out of his face, and breathed in deeply.

Tangled strands stopped his fingers. He hated himself for not removing the ribbon before getting in. He tugged, hearing the frail fabric rip before he finally pulled it free of his hair. Indeed, he had ruined the small piece of torn shirt he had used to tie his hair for ages. He was sure there were still a few bits of cloth in one of his drawers to replace this one. He grabbed a branch and laid the cloth across it for the birds to use.

Then he smoothed his hair, squeezing the excess water out of it along his skull, down his neck, before pulling the rest over his shoulder to wring it out. He preferred mid-back as opposed to the near to the waist or further the others sported.

Except for Doxy. Doxy had a floppy mop that always got into his eyes.

"I need to have a love affair with cold water. At least I get what I need from it," Fedvich muttered to the babbling stream, ducking under again just for good measure. Then he lost himself as he floated on his back, staring up between the leaves to the light clouds covering most of the blue sky.

Chapter 16: Precious Memories

Year of Bertran's Training, 25 years ago

He couldn't breathe at all. His entire body burned, including his mouth, throat, all the way down into the recesses of his lungs. Still, he put one foot in front of the other. The swords, saddles and gear shifted on his back with each step, and he grunted as he fought to keep his feet underneath him. Another breath full of fire filled his mouth, scraped down his throat, and flared to burn him alive from the inside.

Birds chirped. A butterfly dared to flit across his path, making him pause in his pattern. To Fedvich, it seemed he was learning to walk from infancy. Twenty years old, he was a toddler trembling with each footstep, unsure if he could keep his balance.

He kept his eyes on the narrow path in front of him. If he looked up, he'd fall backwards. Not that he knew that from experience or anything.

When the path disappeared into a clearing in three more steps, after a butterfly had nearly toppled him, he scented a fire. Fedvich ventured to raise his gaze. He thanked the gods. He never saw men so beautiful in all his life.

And he wanted to kill all three of them with his bare hands.

Not anytime soon, though. One more step and he let the gear fall off his back. The lightness of only his own weight on his feet created a sensation of flying.

"Good job, boy," Bertran stated while standing up, taking a sip from the earthen mug in his hand. "Want some water?"

Fedvich licked his lips and answered, but nothing came out of his mouth. Why were his lips so rough on his tongue? When had that happened?

"What was that, boy?"

Fedvich's hands tightened into fists at his sides. He worked what little saliva he had into his cotton mouth, "Yes."

"Yes, what?"

"Yes, sir!" Fedvich screamed, but the men only heard a whisper barely louder than the breeze tickling the grass around their campsite on the mountaintop.

"Then go get it." Bertran pointed over the side of the mountain.

The redhead followed that finger, hoping that there was a basin or a bath full of water just beside him he'd missed. His gaze traveled down the rocky slope to where it met another going in the opposite direction. There, far below, between the mountains, was a creek bubbling over gray shale rocks.

He turned toward the other two men, sitting on smooth boulders around the shallow campfire. Surely, they would stop this madman from killing him! He held out a hand, begging, no words coming out.

Then he saw two coins pass from the gray-haired elf, Slayth, to the black-haired man that couldn't be much older than him.

"Kid made it." The elf said with a grin, "Told you he would." He pocketed the coins, saluting Fedvich with another grin and his mug sloshing the contents onto the fire, causing it to spit and hiss.

Fedvich wanted to be that fire so badly in that moment. He turned his gaze back to Bertran. The man remained there, his arms crossed over his chest, and his blue eyes were as sharp as daggers. He hadn't a chance. He was going to die.

If only he still had magic to draw. Fedvich hissed as he turned, one foot in front of the other until he reached the edge of the slope. There wasn't a path. He wasn't about to go back down the one he came up, as he wouldn't get to the creek before nightfall with its winding around.

He could smell water.

Fedvich turned back to the campsite, watching the three men watch him. He could try it. He should try it. He was going to die anyway. Fedvich gathered what strength he had left and launched himself at the fire. He pivoted, dodging the flames and the surrounding stones, to reach out with both hands for the water skin hanging from old Slayth's belt.

Something hard hit the back of his neck. He swore he heard bones crack. His face and hands hit the dirt first, his body sliding them forward with the little momentum he'd built up. Once he stopped, he groaned, blinking dirt out of his eyes to stare at a soft leather boot.

He rolled, looking up at the men from his side, lying at an odd angle that should hurt, but he was already in too much pain to notice any added.

The black-haired man, Regus, held out his hand.

The elf cursed, pulling the coins back out of his pocket and smacking them into the outstretched hand.

"Give him the water." Regus pocketed his coins. "Lasted longer than we expected."

Slayth crouched, lifting him into a sitting position. Then the waterskin was against his lips, and he opened his mouth to let it spill in, quenching the fire one drop at a time.

"It took us two days to get up here. The mountains he crossed to get to that village are rougher, hardly any passes. How did he get from Outpost Owl to that village in a day and a half?" Bertran asked as he sat on his upturned stone.

"He's a witchkin, like he said. Strength like you, or maybe a speed one." Slayth lifted a shoulder, jostling Fedvich.

"Speed," he said hoarsely when Slayth took the skin away from him. He grabbed for it, not hardly done. Fedvich couldn't remember much about the days following the men adopting him into their group. He never explained why he'd been at the village instead of at his post.

They still thought he was an infantryman.

"Easy, eat this first." Slayth held the skin behind his back, holding out a slab of herbal-coated, hard bread in his other hand.

Fedvich did as he was told, swallowing the dry bread in two bites. He held the waterskin in both hands, drinking his fill. He wiped his mouth off on the back of his hand and took another piece of bread from Slayth.

"Why push so hard?"

Bertran shared a glance with the men, then grinned while holding out his hands, palms out. “War puts you in the worst situations. We are ready for them, you should be, too.”

“Even the lord?” Fedvich cast his gaze toward Regus, because he couldn’t even lift a finger to point.

Regus’ grin was wry. “Who do you think he tested that training regimen out on?”

“That explains how you walked on men’s heads before slicing them off.” Fedvich’s eyelids grew as heavy as his body. He swore he still held the gear on his back.

“You will do that, too. Soon. As soon as you finish the rest of the training.”

That made his eyes open. Icy fear gripped his heart. “That wasn’t it?”

Bertran’s chuckle with his twisted smile was answer enough.

Chapter 17: Water Nymphs or is it Mymphs?

This had to be a punishment. Making him walk up the stairs to his room, grab his bow and arrows along with his bracer, then all the way to the pond. He remembered the first time he'd pulled the bowstring and grimaced. Fedvich told him he needed the bracer, especially as a new archer. He hadn't listened. Fedvich had treated the oozing flesh of his forearm and allowed to him complain for days.

Then he'd seen the man shirtless, and then Charn, and the other Seven, and guilt rode him for months. How could he complain about such a minor injury when they all were so scarred? Especially Charn.

Doxy shook his head, clearing his thoughts as he swung himself down the trail with his crutch. Upon reaching the sandy beach, he paused at the pile of clothes and boots on the sand. Fedvich rose out of the water, smoothing his hair back and getting the water out of his face before opening his eyes. Punishment indeed. What was a walk compared to this ache and embarrassment?

All he could do was stare. Fedvich's eyes caught him. He couldn't look anywhere else because if he did, he would do something bad. Something he couldn't come back from because Fedvich would probably get off, then kill him.

Would he die happy?

Yes, yes, he would. He wouldn't have to worry about his family obligations either. He loved his eldest brother dearly, but he doubted Percy would ever marry because of his sensitive nature.

Those bronze eyes closed. Doxy was free to direct his line of sight elsewhere. He did. The water must be cold for the goosflesh all over Fedvich's chest and arms and the way his dark nipples were hard on his tight pectorals.

Then that body was wading toward him. The line going from just above Fedvich's belly button down with each step. And the man didn't pause, didn't care that Doxy was there. Kept walking toward him like some water god of lust.

It wasn't until Fedvich snatched his shirt up and began drying his legs off with it that Doxy realized he had to say something. He needed to use words to disarm the situation. Make them both laugh. He could do that.

"Think I might need to cool off, too." Why was his voice so breathless?

Fedvich had his pants in his hands, readying to put them on when he slid those metallic eyes over. "It's a long walk, especially with something..." he trailed off, his eyes following the missing words down Doxy's form. Stopping somewhere around his waist, then coming back up to affix his gaze on the crutch, "hard."

"Right. I might after we practice." Doxy leaned the crutch against the nearby tree and hobbled over the damp sand to get closer to Fedvich. He had to give the man time to get dressed, so he was exceptionally slow with each step. He kept himself an arm's length away as Fedvich buttoned up, time enough to put on his bracer.

"Well," Fedvich said after they stared at each other for too long. "Are you going to show me what your practice has improved, or do you want to go get your paints? Watching you watching me is rather indulgent."

"I don't have paints!" Doxy cried as his face heated. Right. He shook his head, dragging his eyes away from the half-naked redhead. "What am I aiming at?"

His heart leaped into his throat as something equally jumped below. He imagined bugs crawling over his toes to keep himself contained. Fedvich was walking closer, then he was behind him, his breath hot over Doxy's ear. The long arm lifted, coming even with Doxy's line of sight to point to a tree across the pond.

"There are three targets; one there." Fedvich waited until Doxy acknowledged he saw the wooden shield before lifting to another swinging from a tree limb, and then the third barely visible high in the treetop. "Create your form for me."

Doxy placed his feet shoulder-width apart as he pulled his bow from his shoulder. His knee twinged and throbbed, but he ignored it. Holding the bow in his right and drawing with his left hand to keep the taut string close to his ear, he made his lines as straight as possible. Or so he thought.

"Bring this hand up." Fedvich's fingertips touched Doxy's wrist, holding the bow. His other hand pressed against the middle of his back, "I need the tension to come from here, not your arms," Fedvich explained, his lips still close to Doxy's ear.

He swore his ear was going to burn off the side of his face. Fedvich could probably feel how hard his heart was pounding if he didn't hear it. He hoped the creek rushing along nearby hid any sound that would come from him. Doxy made the changes, waiting for further instructions. He vaguely remembered Fedvich trying to teach him how to use more of his back muscles than his arms the group lesson.

Fedvich slid his hand from Doxy's spine to cup his elbow and bring his arm up level with his shoulder. "Perfect."

His body trembled at the word. He swore Fedvich said it that way to mimic a moan. The man was a bastard and was fully aware of how distracting he was.

"Drop your hold and do it again."

Doxy obeyed the order.

"Better. Watch that elbow." Fedvich tapped Doxy's lowered elbow. "Again."

He steadied his breathing, trying to calm his heart down as he redid his draw. A breeze ruffled his hair, and the hateful stuff fell in his face, tickling his nose. Doxy was about to drop his pull to fix it, when Fedvich's fingers gently brushed across his forehead, pulling the stray locks away.

"You're going to have to learn to focus, Pomm." Fedvich murmured in his ear, those fingers dragging back over the crown of his head, then down to the nape of his neck.

Doxy was pretty sure he was shaking all over with the effort not to lean into that hand and into the body so close to his. "I know." Fedvich's chuckle tickled his ear, and he trembled anew.

"Get an arrow and loose it this time." Fedvich ordered, stepping back.

He pulled an arrow from the quiver strapped to his back and set it correctly.

"Need to work on your speed soon, too."

"Not all of us are experts from the crib like you lot," Doxy muttered, pulling the arrow back and correcting his stance.

"You think the rest of us were born this way?" Fedvich chuckled, crossing his arms over his chest and rocking back on his heels before digging his toes into the sand. "I'll have you know, I was running my business before enlisting."

"Running a business at four years old and enlisting at six?" Doxy asked, making sure the sarcasm held heavy in his words. He drew a breath in, let it out, and repeated as he aimed and let the arrow fly. He cursed when it sank into the edge of the shield.

"I was a hired dick at fourteen and enlisted at nineteen."

Doxy paused in reaching for his next arrow. He looked over his shoulder, trying to gauge whether Fedvich was joking or not. "What's a hired dick?" Was that the same as being a son of Gachent?

"Men who fuck for pay, usually training women to be prostitutes or teaching them to pleasure their rich husbands."

It was the same. He was aware his mouth was hanging open. "Why did you enlist?"

Fedvich lifted a shoulder as he admitted, "Honestly, I didn't."

Chapter 18: Story Time with Fedvich

He sighed, raking his hands through his hair. “Haven’t I told you this already?” Only to raise a brow when Doxy shook his head. “Odd.” He picked a starting point that wouldn’t take too long to explain. “I was born in a village on the border, and only took jobs near it. During the war, I was paid to be entertainment for a few outposts. It was good money, sometimes better than what lords paid to educate their lovers. One night, I woke from a dead sleep as hot as if I was on fire and hearing screams. There was nothing there, the outpost was quiet, cold. I thought it was my village. I grabbed whatever clothes were near and ran across the ridge that was between me and my people. My family.”

His jaw ticked as he remembered that night. He got his bearings, calmed himself by changing his stare from the tree to the flowing, bubbling creek. “It took me two days instead of five because I didn’t stop. My magic was practically drained I used it so much. When I arrived, my village was smoking ashes. The men responsible were dicks deep in whatever women they saved, drunk off our wines, and lazing about in their camp like they hadn’t a worry in the world. I wanted to give them nightmares. I wanted to burn them alive.” He had a twisted smile. “The jacket I stole had two daggers in it. Before I could think, I ran into the middle of that camp, slashing at everything and everyone. It wasn’t long before someone pinned me down because they cut my leg. They took one of those daggers and held it to my throat. I was going to be dead soon, they’d do stuff to me first, of course.” Fedvich lifted a shoulder, knowing it was normal conqueror behavior.

"The sun had set. I swore thunder roared in from the east. But it was Regus, Slayth, and Bertran. I watched those three come in as if they owned the place. Regus just walked out of his saddle while his horse was still at full gallop. Stepped on a guy's helmet and crushed it under his boot-heel as he slid his sword into the neck of another and twisted his wrist to pop off the enemy's head like it was straw. Bertran grabbed another up and used the body like a mace. Slayth... I couldn't see him for the blood spray." Fedvich chuckled at how ridiculous his thoughts were as a kid. "I thought those men were gods arriving to avenge the grandmothers of my home."

Here he slid his gaze back to Doxy. "Bertran found me. Lifted me off the ground like I was nothing, even though I wasn't much smaller than I am now. Regus was right there, in my face, blood pouring off him like he was standing in the rain. Bertran told him I'd killed eight. I was unaware I killed that many, I still think Bertran added a few of his own kills to mine. Regus ripped the patch off the jacket, thinking I was infantry, and said I belonged to him." He gave Doxy a knowing glance, "And here I am."

He watched Doxy take it all in, those eyes of his thoughtful under that mop of hair that kept falling in his face. What he didn't expect was the smile. A smile coupled with a teasing glint that was so rare for the younger man, because as the new member, he was always the one at the brunt of their comedic relief.

"You realize now that they're not gods, right?" His smile was small, but his eyes let slip his humor.

Fedvich couldn't help himself. He threw back his head and laughed. After a few more chuckles, he rounded on Doxy. When the man didn't step away, didn't turn his head, didn't flinch, Fedvich didn't stop until he could bathe in the heat of Doxy's body. "Do I? What makes you think they didn't make me a god?"

"I don't. You were probably a god before them."

Did this man know what he was doing? Pulling the heartstrings to free the monstrous flag of hope within Fedvich's chest before he could keep it hidden and put away. And the worst, making him feel like a god with those wide eyes and parted lips. Did Doxy have the impression that he was looking at a god just then?

Doxy's brows drew together, creating a line in his forehead. "Wait, where was Harry?"

"Not there yet. Harry and I were friends, and I knew he wanted someone to help him take down his father. I brought them together the next month, and we planned the insurrection from there." Doxy's lack of knowledge on this surprised him, honestly. Then again, if he or Harry hadn't told him, none of the others would.

Doxy still stayed put as he asked, "How did you get acquainted with Harry before Regus?"

Fedvich's lips twitched. "I trained his first dominatrix experience, and then I trained him." He watched the surprise fill Doxy's eyes as red filled the man's rounded face. He thought that all of Doxy's softness would be gone by now, two years into him being part of The Seven, but he still had the chubby cheeks and jiggling ass.

"Oh. C-could you train me? Isn't that kind of training making them do stuff you like? I still want to be trained, of course, I just- it would how can I-"

Fedvich drew in a sharp breath through his nose as his body reacted. He'd train Doxy alright. The definitely not-a-god but a ball of lust redhead forced himself to keep his hands away just in case Doxy hadn't a clue what he was saying. He put his hands on his hips. Digging the pads of his fingers into his own pants should remind him to be still. Calm. Not jump the one in front of him like a dog in heat.

"Spit it out, boy."

"I want to learn to make you hard with a look like you do me."

That was it. The breaking point. Gone was the calming cold of the creek. His control strained in a feeble cage. He had to keep still. If he moved one bit, it would be over. He'd make sure Doxy never saw another man as sexy ever again. Doxy Pomm was going to make sure he wanted what he said on his own.

Because if Fedvich had anything to do with the decision, Doxy would cum for him every morning and every night.

"You already own that trick, Doxy. You use it well." He leashed his words, finding better ones than the desperate pleas to fuck. "Archery or fucking?"

Chapter 19: Both? Both. Both is Good

What had he said? What came out of his mouth? Why was Fedvich looking at him like he was going to be the man's next meal and possibly the next? At least he'd be in the man's body one way or another.

He swallowed, forgetting the bow in one hand and the arrow in the other. There was nothing but the redhead in front of him. Fedvich gave him a choice. It was the worst choice. He had to learn archery because he was part of the most prestigious group of warriors known the world over. He had to do his part when the time came for war again. But this was the only way he could get Fedvich to agree to touch him was through sex training. Wasn't it?

"Both," he said, jutting his chin to prove his resolve. He was a fool. Fedvich was going to kill him, right here in the sand. His family would get his body with his dick still half hard, probably.

"Perfect choice."

Doxy moaned because those words were what he needed to hear, and the way Fedvich said them was like honey on a sore throat.

"Do you want to continue with archery, or do you want to get up against that tree?" Fedvich asked, not taking his eyes from Doxy, but tilting his head toward the thick trunk where Doxy's crutch leaned.

"Why do I have to choose?" He didn't understand why a superior was giving him a choice.

"It's going to be rather difficult to hit the target when I fuck you, Doxy."

There it was, the teasing. He hardly minded Fedvich's teasing. Until it was like this. The type that confused him, the words that hinted at promises and desires, but nothing happened.

"Th-then archery. The other tonight." Shame washed over Doxy. He really wanted to throw away the bow and arrow. Take all this training time and be with Fedvich.

"Very well." Fedvich said, his jaw tight. He stepped back twice, his movements slow as if the sand weighed heavily on his feet.

The distance that grew between them seemed to expand into a chasm. Doxy watched Fedvich gaze downward, close his eyes, and puff out his cheeks. Did he dread tonight that badly?

Doxy understood he wasn't a Fedvich, but he was good-looking. He'd made many ladies swoon with a smile. During the hunt, he'd received a handful of handkerchiefs. He probably would have more in his drawer if he'd been the only member of The Seven there. He should learn what he could. Yes, archery. Archery for now, and then sex later. Later he could see if Fedvich hated training him.

Focus on something good. He settled into his stance, knocking an arrow and pulling the string back. "Addy said you helped her during the hunt." From the corner of his eye, he saw Fedvich jerk as if someone had slapped him on the back.

"I did."

"Why did her ass hurt?" He asked, loosing the arrow and cursing as it flew wide.

He turned to face his punishment and saw an all too familiar smile cross Fedvich's face. The one where the man possessed leverage on another. The teasing, sensual grin of a predator catching its prey.

"Are you implying that I gave Adeline a taste of what you're about to enjoy, Sir Pomm?"

He called her by her name, not Miss Pomm. Not even Little Pomm, like he had a habit of doing. "She wouldn't tell me. I wouldn't know if you..." his eyes popped, the meaning behind his words sinking in. "You didn't?!" He pulled back. "Wait. No. Harry would've killed you."

"Would he? He knows how well I teach. A little too well."

Doxy swallowed down the anger that made his heart pound. "Did y-" he couldn't even get it out of his mouth. "Did you train Addy?"

"Why? Going to ask your little sister how I taste?"

His rage snapped, and he launched himself at the other man. His hands were almost around Fedvich's neck when he didn't see him anymore. He saw sand, then hit it, his arm twisted behind him. He spat sand out of his mouth.

"Oh Dox. Doxy, Doxy, Doxy." Fedvich's breath was hot on his ear again. "We really need to work on this acting before thinking thing you do."

Fedvich's weight pressed him further into the sand. Fedvich had moved his hand lower, not twisting it as painfully anymore. Something settled in his palm, hard and cylindrical, while something malleable settled in his fingers. They felt like the pants issued to them; harsh fabrics initially, these softened considerably after being worn to near threadbare.

"She hasn't experienced this sensation, but now you do."

As he spoke, whatever was in his hand slid and pressed, grinding forward. Doxy's face burned before his brain could catch up to his body's reaction. Fedvich was hard for him. Hard and in his hand.

"And I promise you, while she is a close friend now, she definitely hasn't tasted me."

His hand was pulled to their side, and Fedvich moved. Doxy thought he was getting up, but then he felt that rod against his ass. It made his pants give; the cock settling into the crack. He rocked his hips back, wanting more of that.

Fedvich's moan had his own penis throbbing in his pants.

He swallowed hard, moving his body so friction eased the painful erection, but caused it to get worse at the same time.

"Doxy, if you don't want me to take you here, you best still your ass."

"Take me, then."

Fedvich rolled him, he hovered over his body on hands and knees, hair spilling forward to one side, blocking out the tree with the shields in it. Doxy stared up into his eyes, noting the green flecks sparked as if he were about to use his magic. "Careful of your knee," he warned, before letting Doxy take his weight.

Doxy was uncertain about how to position his hands. So he placed them on Fedvich's bare sides, tracing the bumps of his ribs up from his abdomen. He stopped as Fedvich's eyes seemed to flash.

"Doing that is a sure way to get me to ram into you like you're in heat." Fedvich propped himself up on his elbows on either side of Doxy's shoulders. "Didn't you want to taste me?"

He dragged his hand up, knuckles grazing Fedvich's chest until he brushed his fingers over the crimson strands and then cupped the nape of his neck. As he pulled the other man down, he rose to meet him. Who would have thought his lips were so tender? He darted his tongue out to taste Fedvich on his own lips.

But then there was a tongue meeting his.

Fingers slid through his hair before they fisted. He tilted his head as those fingers pulled gently. The tongue delved into his mouth in gentle, slow strokes.

"Doxy!"

Doxy jerked, looking up the trail from where the call sounded. He gasped when Fedvich groaned, but kept lying on him. He stared up, watching those eyes squeeze shut before opening to meet his gaze. "Shouldn't we..."

Fedvich snorted. "Might teach the man patience if we keep going."

He felt an icy hand punch his stomach at the idea of Bertran watching their show. "I don't think that's a good idea." Something crossed Fedvich's features after he said it, and Doxy needed to explain. "What would he think?"

The unknown emotion only deepened before Fedvich smiled wryly. "What indeed?"

Chapter 20: Hung Out to Dry

Bertran had lived too long, that was a given. Fedvich hated himself for thinking such thoughts about a friend, a man who had saved his skin countless times. But he was about to have sex with Doxy for the first time, for the sake of the gods!

First the training that nearly killed everyone, and now this? Fedvich's blood boiled. He cursed and threw himself off Doxy to roll to his feet. He grabbed his boots, shirt, and met Bertran on the trail. The pain in his body was nothing to the frustration pushing him to his limits. "I'm taking tonight and tomorrow off."

"Where are you go-"

"Anywhere else!" Fedvich spat, pushing past the old man. A clamp closed around the back of his neck, and his feet were no longer on the ground. He hissed, kicking out, only to stop as Bertran's glittering blue eyes shot daggers into his own. "What?"

The fingers on his neck flexed before Bertran said, "Do not take out frustrations you build as walls on someone else."

Fedvich stared, the words covering him in guilt. He reached back, tapping the old man's hand. Bertran dropped him. "Still going out."

"Observed." Bertran called out, "Doxy, you are to travel with Slayth to gather our Mister and Missus, and guard them as they visit old friends."

Fedvich's brow twitched. "Only those two?" Bertran's smirk riled him all over again. "See you in a few days, Doxy. I don't remember Regus having that many friends than what he has at home." He refused to look back at his desire as he spoke to him, deciding to stare at a blade of grass beside his bare foot. He was becoming as childish as Harry. Too emotional.

He let the magic lace through his blood, warming him from the inside out. His next step was eight of his normal, the next ten, and the next landed him at the front door of the barracks. Fedvich made his way to the bathing chamber shared by half of the men, washed off after giving himself a much-needed release.

Upon entering his bedchamber, he relaxed a bit more. He would not punch the next person who asked him a question, at least. Getting dressed in his favorite garments made him even better. The pants, made of the softest black-dyed cotton, laced up the side, and only two buttons kept his manhood behind the cloth. His shirt matched, long billowing sleeves and loose laces leaving most of his chest open to whoever wanted to drool over him. He had one boot on when someone opened his door without knocking.

He looked up and gathered himself, for the man's face was a storm.

"So instead of finishing what we started, you're going to town?"

That was a gods damned good question. Fedvich swallowed the saliva before he could make a fool of himself with it. "You're leaving soon. If I know Slayth, you're already late." He watched Doxy's face turn a deeper red.

"Then," Doxy trailed off, then strode across the room to him.

Fedvich fell back when Doxy pushed, his open mouth accosted with tongue and lips. He moaned when Doxy bit his lower lip. His hips rose to meet the hand sliding over his groin. The palm ground into the base of his cock.

"Now you should be as aching as I." Doxy's gaze was sharp, hooded, that face as red as a tomato.

"Wa-" Fedvich started, but Doxy jerked away and turned. "Wait!" Doxy didn't, he even closed the door behind him.

He lay there, staring up at the single rafter crossing his ceiling. He regulated his breathing, willing the throbbing in his cock to lessen in voracity. A review of the day was in order.

When had he gotten so docile? When had Doxy gotten so bold? Was he losing his touch, or had he already lost it? When had he lost the ability to give a man or woman a grin and they automatically stripped for him?

That Doxy Pomm was changing. Perhaps boldness was an ingrained thing they hid well, for Adeline was a dominatrix while being a prim and proper lady. He touched his forehead. Not so proper. What was it with Pomms and lying him flat before he grasped what was going on?

He hadn't had sex with anyone in a year. What was that about? Fedvich knew he grew fixated on things, people especially, but not enough to be celibate for a year. That had to be the problem. He didn't remember a time when his dick had been dry for so long since he turned of age.

Aching indeed. Fedvich sat up, then stood. He raked his hands through his hair, twisting half of it up into a knot and then searching for a shred of cloth in his top drawer. Fedvich tied it into his red strands, knowing it was messy and that half of it would fall by the time he got to town. That was the point. He was sexiest when disheveled.

Another thing he needed to teach Doxy. The man was far too put together. He gritted his teeth as he took the stairs down, picturing several ways Doxy could dress more attractively.

Red-faced, lips parted with a moan, eyes half-lidded and filled with lust as his body...

Fedvich groaned, leaning against the wall beside the front door. He tapped his forehead against his forearm. He had to think of something other than this. What did he usually think about if not Doxy Pomm?

That didn't work. He needed to not think at all. There was only one place he could do that freely.

He flung open the door and glared at the man standing across the threshold.

"The brother I needed to see."

"No."

"You don't even know what I'm going to ask!" Harry cried, holding his palms out, fingers wide.

"To go with me." Fedvich shouldered through the door, bumping Harry out of the way.

"Where are you going?" Harry asked, falling into step beside him.

Anything but this sex fiend. "To town."

"Perfect! Where I was headed, too. Oh see! I already have your horse ready."

Fedvich stopped, staring at his gelding, who lifted his head and whickered a greeting. "No." He turned to Harry. "You go your way, I go mine." Thinking he'd made his point, he finished the walk to his horse and jumped on. He was out of the training grounds and halfway to the lane when Harry caught up with him. "I said no."

"We're going the same way!" Harry cried with a smile, slouching comfortably in his saddle, reins loose in his fingers.

"I hate when Bertran meddles." Fedvich puffed out a breath, telling himself to relax. "Don't you have a wife you need to take whiplashes for?"

"She's fine. Got it in her head to check the house over before Regus and Virsin arrive." Harry didn't hide the bitterness with the last two shards of sentences.

Fedvich was happy to ride in silence, for once, but Harry was not.

"Wanna talk about why you almost kicked Bertran in the balls?"

"Because mine are blue."

Harry chuckled. "And? Is that something new?"

Fedvich cursed Harry under his breath. "Point taken." He looked up at the sky, realizing it was misting rain. "I can still get guys to fuck me, right?"

"Ooooh, this isn't good. You're not going back into the depths, are you?" Harry twisted in his saddle a little to study Fedvich's face. "Yes, you can. Gods, I still want to fuck you."

Fedvich narrowed his eyes at Harry. "That's a given and hardly reassuring."

"Comparing a seasoned professional to someone who's only been wet twice is hardly something to do. It has only been twice still, right?"

Fedvich nodded. It was too easy to get Doxy to spill every secret and detail. He knew exactly how many kisses, touches, and sex encounters the other man had under his belt. Worse, he'd been there for both of the only partnered orgasms Doxy had. He wanted to be there for all of them, the only one there.

"I almost had the third." He inserted to fill the gap in conversation over the plodding hooves and misting rain hitting the tree limbs and leaves above them. An orange glow filled the sky to the west behind the pale clouds. "Today."

Harry's sigh was slow and long. "I woulda kicked Bertran in the balls, too."

Chapter 21: I Love the Smell of Sex in the Morning

Year of Survived Bertran's Training, 24 years ago

Fedvich tilted his head, staring at his jawline while running fingers over it. He followed with his new favorite knife, taking care of the stubble he'd missed in the first round of shaving. In the mirror, he saw the sheets stir behind him. He had little time. Two more swipes told him he was clear of spiky hair.

He studied his face in the mirror, glad that the last hit to his temple had healed. His hair now hid the scar because he kept it long. Another glance behind him in the mirror and he trailed his gaze along the long legs stretching from the sheet, pale as the snow outside.

He watched the sheet get thrown off, pale limbs tangling with those mimicking the color of almonds with a giggle.

"One more, Master Fedvich?" He asked the Fedvich in the mirror with a whisper.

His name spoken in a deep baritone, as a dark hand reached for him, and the giggling woman saying it right after while straddling the very naked and ready male in bed with her. He turned, tossing his knife onto his neatly folded pants on the chair in the corner. The stark contrast of pale against dark was a wonder to behold. Fedvich was certain the duo would go far.

Not just because of his tutelage, which tripled their appeal, but because of their sheer elegance.

He wished he could have gotten paid for training the two. But he had not yet gained recognition in this city. Fedvich let the man draw him into a kiss while the woman licked his cock. With the right clientele, these two could buy the city within a year.

Thick, wet fingers slid between his cheeks, working the lube around and into his hole. “Perfect,” he murmured, curling his fingers in the blonde curls, pulling her up from kissing his cock to tasting his tongue.

As if reading his mind, the duo moved into position. She lay on her back. While stretching her legs wide, she fondled her own breasts as she waited for the dicks to get into place. Fedvich relaxed himself, dipping his head down to slide his tongue through her wet slit. He moaned against her clit as the head of their partner’s dick pushed inside him, causing her to moan in turn.

He brought his fingers up, sliding two into her as he watched large black balls brush up against his rear and own sack. Fedvich lifted his head, using the strength his training beat into him, he pulled her down the sheets onto his cock.

In three thrusts of that long dick inside him, he was ready to release, but he tethered his pleasure. “Customer cums first.” Fedvich breathed between their bodies slamming together, “Unless it’s me, then ladies first.”

When the ball sack started slapping his ass, he knew he was done for. But when the man pulled his head back by his hair, he trembled all over. Luckily, the woman jerked, crying out her orgasm as she tightened around his cock. The man thrust into him again, and he lost it, jerking out of her just in time to spill his seed between them.

The door flew open.

Fedvich stared wide-eyed, his heart dropping into his stomach, icy hands skated up his spine even as warm seed spilled into him with a few harsh jerks.

“Think you can be ready in twenty?” Those midnight eyes never moved from his.

He nodded, still poised over the woman with his flaccid cock in his hand while the other manhood slid out of him.

“Good. Downstairs in twenty.” Regus ordered, closing the door behind him. Not a bang, not a half-hearted click, the door closed normally. Was that a good sign? Or a bad sign? He’d never seen Regus watch sex, or during sex, or anything of that nature. What had the expression on his face been?

"Fuck me."

"Just did." The deep baritone answered as the man flopped beside them on the bed, stretching out.

"Was that your daddy?" The woman purred, squeezing him with her pale thighs.

"No, my dad would be proud of me if he were still alive. That one, he might kill me." Fedvich swallowed, looking between the two of them. "It's been a wonderful, lovely experience. Remember me kindly." He leaned down, kissing each of them before jumping off the bed.

He washed himself off in the basin, then pulled on his clothes as quickly as he could, listening to the chattering reassurances from the woman still in his bed.

They'd been in this city for two weeks. Preparing for a pivotal move in this war that would kill them if they failed. They were already behind enemy lines, and here he was fucking around. Literally.

His boots were a nuisance; he missed the sandals and wraps he used to wear. Fedvich grabbed the fur-lined jacket and gave the duo one last kiss. He needed it; they didn't. The stairs were a blur as he ran down them, hooking his hand around a support post to swing down to the next set. He kept running down the hall once he arrived, skidding to a stop in front of the open door of their meeting room.

Looking in the door, down the length of the table, he met that dark gaze. If those were the eyes he would stare into while taking his last breath... No, he didn't want to die. Fuck that.

He entered the room, closing the door behind him and nodding to Slayth, then Bertran on either side of Regus. "Morning." His mouth was so dry that the word barely came out. It reminded him of his training days, and his body gave a cramping twinge all over in remembrance.

"Glad you could join us," Regus muttered, taking a folded parchment out of his sword's sheath. He flattened it out on the table, the other two men holding the corners down as all three leaned in to study it.

He would not die? He could live with that. Fedvich moved further into the room, standing beside Bertran, the safer bet of the three. Bertran was emotionless when it came to physical acts other than inducing death in others.

"Harrick sent this message." Regus pulled another sheet of paper out of his breast pocket, tossing it to Fedvich.

He picked it up, noting his hand shaking as if he were a leaf desperately clinging to its branch in a storm. He read it. Harry's handwriting was terrible, so it would take him a while.

"Out loud, boy," Slayth ordered.

"Right." For the first time in several years, his face grew warm.

"Hello gentlemen, and dearest friend,

I hope this finds you ready for the greatest night of our lives. You shall not find the sun in the east, but its light will shine bright in the northwest. The parapets are great for seeing the sunset, if only you could climb them and hold on long enough. There is not a better view of the kingdom, I assure you, except maybe from the queen's balcony. She has a swing there, perfect for sunset dates. Just be sure to get permission, or you will have to be out by the first star, the beautiful Tiarna of the winter skies, makes her appearance. Be sure to inspect the bookcase while you wait for the view. My favorite is the Tales of Sons of Gachent, though our dearest friend knows all about that. Take a torch, the castle, once the sun sets, grows as dark as night, especially in the west wing. Perhaps you could gaze at the moon from the balcony at the end, do you know the moon will be full tomorrow night? There you have it, perfect views for perfect gazing at our celestial beauties. I look forward to meeting you under the moon.

Yours in friendship and truest loyalty, Harrick Tearney, Seventh Prince of Serland.

"That's all." He wasn't about to read the postscript, for that was for him and him alone.

Except Regus had pulled this out of his pocket. No envelope. How screwed could he be in one day?

"Is it?"

Fedvich met Regus' gaze, "Sir?"

"Are you sure that's the end of the letter?"

"Isn't something about another bedroom?" Slayth asked, not looking up from drawing lines on the map and telling Bertran the measurements. They were assessing the time it would take to go from one point to the next to aid Harry in his treachery.

They had read the letter. "Why don't we talk about this? I can explain. I assure you I am not-"

"An infant?" Slayth asked, one side of his lips pulling up as he straightened from hovering over the map.

"Infantry," Bertran corrected before adding, "that he is not, nor ever was."

"Definitely not a virgin." Regus added, taking a sip of his steaming mug before placing it down on the corner Bertran abandoned holding when he began his calculations.

Fedvich thought he was watching some game between the trio, and he was the target. With each look, his heart shuddered and stomach turned. He'd kept this secret for three years. Three years and one fuck lost him everything.

"No, I'm not an infant. Infantry." Fedvich closed his eyes, cursing the way Slayth belittled everyone that wasn't Bertran. "I was at Owl Outpost. I was paid to do my job. I'm good at it."

"Teaching our infantry to make infants? I would imagine so. With your newly gained stamina these days, you could double your profits. How much did you make last night?" Regus watched Bertran scratch numbers below the lines Slayth drew. "That damn parapet is going to be our death."

"Agreed, fully exposed up there and not even in nightfall." Slayth rubbed the back of his head, unsettling his silvery hair.

Fedvich shook his head, as if he could clear the rambling thoughts. Not only was he trying to follow the plan, but he was also saving his own skin. "I wasn't working last night. I don't have a name here and I've been out of business for three years."

"Well, after this tonight, if we don't die, you could have time to start anew. All at night, of course. It can't interfere with training." Regus' gaze was on Fedvich.

"You won't throw me out?"

Bertran snorted, "After all the work I put into you? You're worth at least twenty years of helping keep this one alive," he pointed at Regus. "And conquering our enemies."

"You're not disgusted and going to stone me?" Fedvich had heard the stories from men like him in the surviving major cities. Sons of Gachent shouldn't sully the prim ladies, and the men didn't want them, not at all.

Slayth shook his head. "None of us here have a kink like that."

"I don't have any kinks." Bertran added in his droll monotone.

"You're okay with me-"

"Fucking across the lands at every port and post? Sure." Regus shrugged.

"He's pretty enough to make everyone shoot dry." Slayth chuckled and shook his head, then pointed his pencil at him. "I used to partake of dicks, but I fancy women, one woman, now. Don't get any ideas if you have a dry spell."

Regus lifted a shoulder as he stated, "If I get desperate enough, we might have a go."

Fedvich snorted. "Sir, sorry, but after seeing what you do by merely stepping off your horse onto someone, I'm not sure I can survive you."

The men chuckled, going back to the map to hash out a few details. Fedvich had a nagging thought in the back of his mind. "I've wondered this for a while, but why is Regus so special? He's a baron."

Slayth sighed, stretching and popping his back. “He’s the king’s cousin, but other than that... he has a face everyone wants to smash.”

Regus nodded, “I am ugly enough.”

Fedvich stared at the baron, knowing then that the man was blind. Slayth and Bertran both cleared their throats, and Fedvich looked between them, both men shaking their heads. There are some things he shouldn’t correct.

Chapter 22: Redheads Not Allowed

"Boy, if you turn around in that seat one more time, I will tie you to one of those draft horses."

Doxy straightened automatically, back stiff. He gripped the reins for a moment, wondering if he had reacted quickly enough for old man Slayth's satisfaction. He cut his eyes to the side, letting out the breath he was holding.

"Why do you think Fedvich is going to come after us? You tell him I was gonna teach you a few things?" Slayth's smirk was wicked, even in profile.

His heart dropped, "How did you know it was Fedvich I was looking for?"

"Because the two of you drool ovcr one another like teenagers hungry for their first. That's how."

Doxy snorted, "I'm the only one drooling." He caught a measured, yet unreadable look from Slayth out of the corner of his eye. "What?"

"I knew you were dramatic, but I didn't take you to be blind, too."

Doxy stared at the man, rocking with the wagon carrying supplies for the couple. Apparently, being on vacation for two and a half weeks had been enough for Virsin to wear all of her dresses she'd packed twice over, and she was tired of them. At least that was the excuse, part of it, Regus used to summon Slayth and Doxy to their side.

The other sentence to the letter stated Regus wanted to visit old friends near the ocean, a village called Gachent.

The problem was, Regus didn't have any friends other than The Seven. That's what Slayth and Bertran said after reading the letter. Doxy thought the old men were overreacting.

Regus was as secretive as any of his acquaintances. He could have friends.

People who didn't mind being scared out of their wits with his glares every five seconds.

Like Slayth, who was another competent at wielding deadly glares and piss-inducing smiles.

"Then, old man, tell me how I'm blind. I'm not dramatic." Doxy hated how his face always followed his words. He realized he was doing what his sister called pouting.

"Fedvich wants you."

"He wants everyone." Doxy countered.

"Not like he wants you, boy."

He shook his head. "Then why hasn't he made his move?"

Slayth's laugh echoed through the trees, and back to them. "You really are an idiot."

"Am not!" Doxy let out before sobering with Slayth's raised brows. "When did he make a move?" Other than the kiss from before. But that had been his move, hadn't it? The whole day had been Doxy taking initiative, not Fedvich.

"He can't. Not with you shooting him down with every comment you make after he suggests it."

That didn't make any sense. "He's never suggested it."

"Boy, would you ask him if he wanted a fuck in a room full of others?"

Doxy's cheeks burned, "No." Slayth's gaze spoke volumes more than words ever could.

Slayth rode ahead, checking the road and surrounding area, always within earshot and eyesight. It gave Doxy time to think. Today. Had anything Fedvich done or said meant he wanted sex? Other than all the things after they made the agreement. Nothing came to mind.

Not Fedvich calling their training session a date. Not mentioning that he was imagining fucking someone that night and then promising to train him. He hadn't made a comment about changing plans with anyone. The why behind Fedvich bathing in the creek instead of following him to the barracks for a proper wash... was he the cause of the cold bath?

There were the times throughout the year that Fedvich teased him. But the man teased everyone. He wasn't a special case there. Slayth was wrong.

The old man rode back to him, taking his place beside the wagon, making his horse plod along with the team.

"He's never offered. You're wrong."

Slayth grumbled under his breath, hooking his leg around his saddle horn and sitting as if he were relaxing on a large chair instead of on the back of a horse. "Remember him asking if you needed help bathing after twisting that knee?"

Doxy nodded, "Yeah, of course." He stared at Slayth as the old man stared at him. "It was nice of him."

"Hopeless," Slayth said the word like it were his favorite curse. He dug into his saddlebags, taking out two pears. He tossed one to Doxy before taking out his knife and carving a little slice off. "Do us all a favor when we get back; you walk right up to that narcissistic bastard and stick his dick in your mouth."

His face flamed again. "I... I dunno if I'm any good at that."

"Son, that's between you and him. If you were after a woman, I'd talk all about that. All I know with dicks is what I like, and you are not privy to those details."

Doxy slumped and picked apart the memory of Fedvich saying he'd bathe him in his head. The redhead had definitely been teasing; he had that grin. With his perpetual gorgeous smile and a touch of sarcasm, he would lift Doxy's hopes each time.

Now that he thought about it, he couldn't imagine Fedvich bathing anyone unless he was getting off, too.

Fedvich said that he needed to work on thinking instead of taking action. With Fedvich, he thought. Perhaps too much. He certainly didn't act. Until today.

"Why did Regus want me instead of Fedvich? Isn't Gachent his village?"

"That's precisely why Regus doesn't want Fedvich," Slayth answered readily. "If there is something precious to you, you don't think straight."

Doxy eyed the old man, finally taking a bite of the pear. It wasn't his favorite fruit, as the flesh always created sand in his mouth. "What didn't I catch this time?"

Slayth chuckled, finishing his pear with another slice and tossing the core into the woods beside the road. He ate the bite off his blade. "Regus has news of trouble from there."

"I'm not going to be any help."

"You don't have to be. You and that wagon are bait."

Doxy felt his stomach drop, "Oh." He pictured the two lines of the letter in his head. "How did you get all of that from ten words?"

Slayth licked the juice off his knife before putting it back. "Ever heard the duchess complain about her dresses?"

"No."

"Ever seen Regus ride in a wagon?"

Doxy was seeing a few things between the lines. "No."

"What am I good at?" Slayth asked with a raised brow.

"Killing, stealth, and cleaning up blood."

"Now then, put all that together, boy."

Although the wagon lacked a canvas cover, tarps wrapped the trunks, clearly displaying their number and size. "There's a band of thieves in Gachent."

"Good job." Slayth clapped slowly.

Doxy gritted his teeth to keep from being hateful. He didn't need to die this day. Especially not when he had a dick to suck when they got back.

Chapter 23: Sucking Weeds and Old Friends

Fedvich stepped into one of his favorite places. He took in the musk and smoke scent with a deep breath through his nose. The haze limited the line of sight through the establishment, and few lanterns were lit.

"Vichy!"

He grinned at the owner, catching the slim form in his arms when she threw herself at him. "Didn't think you would remember me, Wyn."

"It has been too long." Wyn's full red lips formed a pout as she drew back from her hug. "I was beginning to think you dead. Haven't heard a thing about you."

"It's been quiet." Fedvich admitted, loosening his hold to let her slide down him to regain her footing. When she wrapped her arms around his waist, he chuckled. The woman was skin and bones, and tried to make up for it by wearing billowing silks. Each touch was unforgiving. "How's business?"

"Dwindling." Wyn rested her chin on his sternum, glaring up at him. "I don't have a showman anymore."

Fedvich raised his eyebrows. "Oh? I remember training plenty."

"Training and being you are two completely different things." Her spidery hand patted his cheek. Then she turned, spinning once to her desk. "What should you desire today?"

"My usual relax and sleep concoction." He followed her to the desk, a tiny, spindly thing that took up very little of the corner.

"I thought that would be it." She reached into a drawer, pulling out two hand-wrapped cigarettes and a small tonic glass complete with a dropper. "You haven't been here in nearly a year, what have you been doing to let loose?"

"Nothing. That's the problem." Fedvich stated, taking the bottle and emptying the dropper until only the tip held what he needed. He put it under his tongue, holding the medicine there and willing it to work quickly. He gave her the bottle back and slipped two coins from his pocket to place in her hand.

She held his hand and the coins. "I have two-"

"Not tonight."

She took the coins. "Very well. I'm afraid your usual room is taken, but the one next to it is free."

He nodded, taking the smokes before parting the sheer curtains that separated the front of the house from the back. The foyer of the old family home was now an open lounge room. Pillows and beds, sheets and bedspreads were strewn haphazardly between curtains that did little to create partitions. Chaises and couches circled glass contraptions with hoses coming out of them to metal ends.

"Fedvich!" a familiar voice called.

He followed the sound to his right and blew a kiss to the dancing woman before taking the carpeted stairs up to the second floor. Few rooms had activity, doors open to the hall, beckoning those who passed by to partake of the drugs and drink within.

His favored room was at the end of the hall to the right, what used to be the master chambers when the structure still housed its lord and lady. They gambled their riches away, leaving their only daughter the house and debt. Luckily, Wyn began her business dealing drugs to the elite. When he began visiting, they struck a bargain all those years ago. Wyn dealt in pleasure also ever since.

He paused at the door to the room next to it, but noticed the doors were open enough to let someone peek in. That was an invitation. Fedvich shrugged and entered his room.

Clever Wyn. Fedvich left the doors open ajar, taking a match from the table beside him to light his second treatment. He let it fill his lungs and held it before letting the smoke flow from his nose.

Silks hung from the ceiling in all colors. There were no couches or beds in the chamber. Large plush pillows covered the floor, smaller ones were mixed in, and blocks of wood lent something to lean the pillows on if a backrest was desired.

A naked, pot-bellied lord sat on a pillow, reclining against another as he sucked on the metal pipe. The two in the silks held his glassy gaze. No tent under his belly.

Fedvich watched the jerky movements of the dancers. While the woman had legs for days and apple-sized tits, she had little grace and no comprehension of sex appeal. The man, barely such, was too fascinated by wrapping his cock in silk and humping it.

He turned, peering out into the hall and smiling at a Wyn who was pretending not to have followed him up. "Is Quin here?"

"Of course! But he's with someone."

"It doesn't matter, bring them both."

Some things never changed. He could easily fall into his habits here again. Refilling his trunks with gold and silver on top of what he had earned as a mercenary. No, he was a mercenary these days. He took another slow drag, catching the fish-eyed gaze of the lord and motioning for him to leave.

Sluggishly, the lord pushed and rolled himself to his feet and meandered his way out the door.

"That was our supper!" The boy cried, still not bothering to unwrap his member.

"You're harder than he is." Fedvich observed dryly, "He wouldn't have passed either of you a single coin. Get out of my silks."

"Who are you, hm?" The woman had her hands on her hips, standing amid the shimmering cloth.

"Your guarantee." He sensed the opium slip him some calm finally. He smiled to himself as he made his way to the center of the room. Fedvich arranged the pillows and himself how he liked, dropping his arm across the back of his backrest as he stretched out.

"Fedvich!" was his only warning before being straddled.

"You have new rings." Fedvich chuckled, watching the silver, gold, and jewels flicker in the candlelight as Quin's hands fluttered around him as if the whore was unsure of where to touch.

"Yes! Do you like them?"

"Hm." Fedvich glanced toward the door. "Where is your customer?"

"Oh, he squirted in five seconds and then passed out." Quin waved a hand dismissively. "I've missed you!" The man bounced in his lap while sporting the devilish grin Fedvich taught him.

"As I have you." He replied, taking another drag and letting everything roll loose with a full-body stretch. "Quin, why haven't you been teaching since I've been gone?"

Quin whimpered, riding the stretch while roaming his hands up under Fedvich's shirt. He froze at the question, his bright blue eyes widening. "Was I supposed to?"

Perhaps there was something to that saying about brains leaking out with each ejaculate. He slid his fingers up Quin's shoulder, cupping the back of his neck and bringing him down. If he stuck his tongue out, he could lick Quin's bottom lip. "Yes, Quin, you were."

"O-ooh," Quin trembled, eyes zeroed in on Fedvich's lips.

He was aware of Quin's arousal pressed into his abdomen. He still had it. "Remember where to begin?" He watched Quin nod, the man's mouth open, waiting for the kiss. "Now then, get to it." He dropped his hand, bucking his hips to dislodge the other.

With a whimper, Quin rolled, crouching beside Fedvich. "After... can I have a prize?"

"Perhaps if you do well enough."

Fedvich watched the trio, finishing his first and flicking it to a bare spot on the wooden floor.

"I hate these places."

He grunted as he lit his next cigarette and made sure it was set before looking up at Harry. "Didn't have to come."

"I can't leave you alone in this den of iniquity." Harry sat down beside Fedvich and watched the session before them.

Fedvich snorted. “You’re one to talk. Every room you enter turns into a den of iniquity.”

Harry took the rolled smoke from Fedvich’s fingers. “Says the one who taught me everything I know.” He then closed his eyes as he partook of the gentle drug.

“Hmm, I did.” He couldn’t help but smile at those memories. Like the one learning to make the lady in the room wet. He then watched Quin bound to him like a puppy. “Well?”

“They are on their first lesson.” Quin waved hands toward the duo as he landed on his knees between Fedvich’s. “Oh, you’re new!” He smiled sweetly at Harry, his eyes ruining the flirtation as they darted from one to the other. “Are you brothers?”

“From different fathers.” Their old joke. It was too difficult to explain their closeness to strangers.

“Can I have prizes from both of you?” Quin clapped his hands excitedly.

“No, just me,” Fedvich said after Harry gave him a glare. He popped the buttons open on his pants, pulling out his flaccid cock, then returned to his relaxed pose. He snaked his hand into Harry’s locks and pulled, making the man grin.

“Hm, that’s a first.” Quin and Harry both muttered at the same time.

“Shut your mouth around it,” Fedvich growled to Quin, then pointed at Harry, “You can go suck on your wife.”

“Gladly, once you’re done.”

“Give me one minute,” Quin said with a sly grin before dipping his head to take Fedvich in.

Fedvich snorted, then had to study, as his cock throbbed with a single unfamiliar sensation. “I didn’t teach him that.”

Harry chuckled. “Guess the student has become the teacher this day.” He leaned over, kissing Fedvich deeply.

Chapter 24: Being Tight is Not Always a Good Thing

Year of Survival of Bertran Training, 24 years ago, less one night

"Ah, pardon."

Fedvich had that as a warning before a foul stench filled his nose. "Gods!" He nearly lost his grip on the thick rope.

"Hold steady and hush up there!" Bertran whispered harshly, then muttered, "Shouldn't have ordered all that protein for supper."

He waved the air in front of his face, hugging the rope with legs and one arm. He looked down, big mistake. They were closer to the top than to the bottom. "Why am I below you?" He frowned at the white fog coming from his mouth. It was too cold to be hanging off the side of a castle.

"I'm always a top when it comes to fellow sword wielders." Slayth pulled himself up at a steady pace. "Besides, thought you might enjoy the view before you meet the prince in his bedchambers."

"Shh!" The sound was as bad as Regus' normal orders.

Fedvich tried to peer around Slayth to see if Regus was leaning over the edge of the wall to shush them, or if he'd pulled some other mysterious magic. He swore the man was a witchkin and in denial. Just like how he also denied his looks.

He knew he was the prettiest of the four, but Regus was certainly second.

Slayth pulled himself over the edge ahead of him. Fedvich made quick work of the rest of the length of rope and fell onto the wall. He huffed a breath, rolling himself up to his feet before Bertran stepped on him. He pulled the rope back up, coiling it in a tight circle at his feet.

"One step down," Slayth muttered, reaching to place his hand around the hilt of his longsword.

Regus moved forward, swiftly pulling the sword nearly as wide as Fedvich from his back. In one swing he beheaded the two guards huddled around a torch for warmth. He then looked back at them, his brows raised. "Do I need to send you an invitation?"

Slayth hissed, "Ass."

Bertran moved forward, passing both of them, "You're the one that raised him."

"As did you." Slayth shot back, breath pluming in front of him.

Fedvich took up the rear, turning his back to the men and following them through listening to their footsteps. Plus, the parapet was a straight walk into another wall. He grunted, bumping into Slayth before he stopped. He turned, looking at the next rope.

Leaning slightly over the edge, he spotted a balcony. He straightened, a chill screeching through his body. "Tell me there is another balcony under us, we just have to swing a little and hop down. Right?"

"Time to be like a monkey."

"I've never seen monkeys!" Fedvich spat, then cupped his hands in front of his mouth to breathe on his fingers to warm them. He watched the sun inch further down behind the horizon, putting the city beneath them in long shadows.

"Watch." Slayth pulled Fedvich to the edge.

Regus was on the rope, hand over hand going down, then he put his feet on the wall and ran back toward the parapet. Ice shards fell from his footprints. He paused, bouncing on his toes, before running forward as fast as he could, then pushing off and swinging. His clothes made him whistle through the air before he let go of the rope and rolled onto the balcony. He stood, motioning them to hurry.

Fedvich closed his eyes and tried to still his rabbiting heart with a few deep breaths. "It's just like sneaking out of a mansion."

"Of course. Except hundreds of feet higher, ice on the walls, and gods know what's underneath all that fog below us."

There were times he truly hated Bertran.

Slayth went, graceful as ever. Propelled by farts. Fedvich muttered to himself the whole time he let himself down the length of the rope. He looked up, thinking he was down far enough. He ran back on the wall, hanging onto the rope for dear life. What color were the stones of the castle under all the white, glistening stuff? He'd never figured his ass could become so tight.

He dug his heels in, then ran forward, half slipping, half hitting his footholds. Fedvich took more time on the wall than the others, then pushed off. Ice shards in the wind pelted him as he watched the balcony fly toward him.

Fedvich couldn't let go. He caught Regus' eyes as the rope brought him to the edge of the balcony. He sensed the momentum wane. Squeezing his eyes shut, he willed his hands to loosen.

The rope jerked, and he opened his mouth to scream, but held it. He stared down into the narrowed eyes of his lord and sighed. Saved.

"Get. Your. Ass. Down." Regus words slid through gritted teeth.

Fedvich scurried down the rope. As soon as his feet were on the stone of the balcony, Regus threw the rope back. "Forgive me." He shook his head, leaning down on his knees. "I can master the silks now. If I survived that... I can definitely master them."

"Silks?"

Fedvich stared up at Slayth. "It's... you have to see it."

After Bertran landed, the men entered the chambers of the deceased queen through the wide-open doors. Fedvich strode to the bookcase, after eyeing the sun setting behind the city from the balcony windows on the other side of the room. He ran his fingers over the spines, then found the green leather-bound book. He grinned, pulling it, and then handing it to Slayth. "Page twenty-six."

The bookcase slid to the side after much grinding and clacking. Regus cursed the noise, sword poised and pointed at the entrance to the chamber.

"This has nothing to do with silk." Slayth turned the book to its side.

"No, but your wife will enjoy it."

"Put that away!" Regus hissed, jerking his chin toward the hidden entrance to a narrow hall.

Fedvich grabbed a lantern, lighting it with the matches beside it. He entered the hall, the men quickly filing in behind. Grunting, he turned sideways, holding the lantern ahead of him as he adjusted to a sidewinder gait. The air was stagnant, but warm. He glanced behind him, watching the other three men holding their breath to make themselves narrow enough to pass. "What was Harry thinking taking us to the ass of the castle?"

Bertran added gruffly, "One of us should be right at home."

"The lantern light brings out the gold in your eyes," Slayth said in a warbling high pitch.

Fedvich groaned. "Trust me, it's the green you want to see, and you have to be in *me*, not in the sphincter of a castle."

A small light lined the bottom of the hall ahead. He rushed toward it, pushed the bookcase open and fell out. Breathing in the fresh air. He looked around the room, catching sight of a familiar face.

"Fedvich." Harrick grinned, getting up from reclining in a chair to stride over and grab his face.

Fedvich took the kiss readily enough. Harrick had been his best student, and the only one he considered a friend. Though the armory strapped to the prince was a new appearance. He pulled back, patting Harrick's chest. "Ready to kill your father?"

Harrick moaned, closing his eyes. "Yes, all night yes."

"Well, that wasn't quite the scene I was expecting after hearing a moan like that."

"Me neither, especially not those." Regus pointed to two bodies behind Harry.

Harry turned. "Ah, those. I would introduce you to my older brothers, but they're dead."

Fedvich's stomach turned at how nonchalant Harry was being, before he reminded himself of the things the two had done. He nodded when Regus ordered Harry to lead the way. He pulled his short swords from his thighs, finding comfort in the familiarity of them in his hands. It also scared him. Swords were comforting?

Harry's animalistic smile was such an odd thing, it sent chills all over his flesh.

He watched his favorite student fling open the doors before striding out. Harry reached to his side, coming back with a handful of throwing daggers. The seventh prince greeted the two guards before flinging two of the daggers at them. The metal imbedded in their throats.

"Open those doors. The king is mine. The rest are yours."

Slayth and Bertran flowed forward on silent feet. They covered the length of the wide, carpeted hall, bare of decoration except for a single painting covering most of one wall. The family. All forty-six of them, including the four wives and five concubines. Fedvich followed close behind the older gentlemen, noting Harrick's presence behind him, and Regus beside him.

Slayth opened one side, Bertran the other. Fedvich tried to take in the chaos that was already before him. Guards stood shoulder to shoulder along each wall. In the center, a single throne filled with furs. At the base, a man crouched behind a woman, rutting.

Fedvich met his eyes, noting the woman was limp, and his blood boiled.

The king stopped, staring at them. "Guards! Bring me my ungrateful son's head!" His laugh echoed in the chamber. "You even brought the whore I bought you for your first time!"

If the secret hadn't been out before, he'd have some explaining to do in the middle of killing.

Fedvich pivoted to the side, slashing through the opening between the golden helm and the plate armor of the guard's chest. He stepped over the body of another woman, once dressed in blue if the surrounding shreds were any indication. Sinking his other dagger into the man screaming at him while running toward him, right under the chest plate in his soft belly.

Noticing all the guards running toward the center of the room, he turned to find out why, before throwing another guard down with his own momentum. He stepped on him, bending to cut the throat open. Fedvich looked back up in enough time to see five armored bodies fly in an arc, blood spilling from the gashes in their armor.

Regus had to be witchkin.

He grunted with the sharp pain in his side. He looked down, seeing a pin sword covered in a stripe of blood. “Well, that’s not nice.” He punched the guard, then stabbed him in the eye when the guy didn’t move enough. Fedvich remembered not to touch his side. That led to slippery fingers, and one couldn’t fight well that way.

Their voices were in his head in every battle.

“Did you teach that one manners?” Slayth called from the other corner, a swirl of blood hiding him.

“What in gods fucking is that?” Harrick cried.

“Blood elf. Say it with me: Blood. Elf.” Slayth parted the surrounding whirlpool, glaring at Harry. “To your left.”

Harry whirled, wrapping a whip around the attacker’s neck while kicking his knees out from under him. He jerked the leather, bones cracked, and the guard fell limp. In the next instant, he slashed the whip down; the end leaving a welt under the king’s left eye.

Fedvich returned his attention to his corner of the room. The guards were slow. Their armor too heavy, their bodies too untrained. It was as if he was watching them move through water. Another two whiplashes snapped behind him and the king’s scream rang in his ears as he stabbed an enemy in the neck.

“Thrilling, isn’t it?”

Fedvich’s brows drew together. “No?”

Bertran cackled.

The man was mentally unstable. He saw the folly of having short swords against slow opponents. Fedvich sheathed them, ducking a wide swing. He pulled the bow off his shoulder, stringing it as he mule-kicked another behind him, then kicked him in the head when he went down. After a string test he then hooked an arrow from the quiver on his back to it. He sprang up the corner, and perched on the decorative crown molding halfway up a pillar.

In quick succession, he downed four guards, arrows to their right eyes. He took his next arrow, shooting it through the jugular of the one he'd kicked down. With another arrow he shot, missed his mark, but it skewered the next guard's cheek. Fedvich shot down four more guards.

"Out!" Slayth called to him, and Fedvich cursed when his next reach grabbed air. He dropped and rolled to a crouch, then straightened. He strode to the first four he downed, yanking the arrows free. Only two had the arrowheads and one of them had a melting eye and mucus stuck to it.

"Why don't you use the sword?"

Fedvich shot the guard Bertran was shaking in his right hand. He grinned when Bertran cursed him. "Why don't you?"

"I like this banter in battle." Harry's laugh was dark. His father was stepping backward, throwing whatever guard remained upright toward his son. Harry pushed them away, calmly following his father through the room with steady steps.

Had the king had pants on while fucking the dead woman?

Fedvich shook his head, clearing that image out of his mind. The tyrant had pants on now, thank the gods. Red scales were forming here and there on the bare chest, too. He frowned, the remaining guards were fleeing or in the process of taking their last breath via one of the other three in the room.

Bertran happily declared, "Don't worry, boy. This little room is an appetizer. The actual battle is when we try to get out."

"Right. I know." Fedvich swallowed, his stomach turning. He pulled the rest of his arrows free. He discarded the ones whose heads remained in skulls. Four. Someone needed to invent better arrows. He cleaned them off on a guard's cheek before putting them back in his quiver.

Whiplashes still sounded at regular intervals. He looked up, watching the blood flowing to Slayth slow, then drop. The pool of red around the blood elf thickened and oozed outward slowly. Bertran leaned against a wall, checking his nails and digging blood and flesh out of them with someone else's fingernail still attached to a severed hand. Regus was lovingly cleaning his sword with a tattered fiber cloth, his eyes on the prince and king.

"Please!" the king begged for the hundredth time. He screamed when Harry whipped his hand, the ring and pinky finger falling off. He stumbled back, clutching his stubs, then tripped over a body and splayed on the floor.

The whip came down on his crotch; the pants ripped and blood spurted. Harry didn't stop with one. The king screamed and cried curses with each hit, trying to twist away, only to be whipped on a thigh or ass and his body instinctively rolling back to protect the fresh wound.

The king curled up in a fetal position at the entrance. Dark ruby-red scales erupted along his back as the man elongated. A screaming growl shook the room.

Harry stepped over him, jerking him up by his pale red hair. When his father opened his mouth to scream or curse, Harry grabbed his tongue. Holding him up by the slippery organ and shaking off the hair of his newly freed hand. He slit his father's tongue and lips off with his dagger, then shoved them into the open, gurgling maw as his teeth sharpened into the predator within.

Fedvich looked away as Harry began carving into the man's chest.

"Need the head as bait, and proof." Regus stated calmly, watching the scene unfold before him as if it was nothing new.

"Done," Harry said, switching his dagger for the sword on his back. He hacked, then held up his father's head, half human, half dragon in a twisted glassy state of death. "Shall we?" He asked, motioning to the door with his father's dripping head.

Chapter 25: Bait and Tackle

He found being bait to be overrated. Not long after they picked up Regus, they he was put to work making the load look enticing. It was hot. The wagon seat was part of his body. And he swore if the brown draft horse didn't stop farting, he was going to puke.

He leaned to the right, trying to get a sniff of fresh air, but there was only more stench. Doxy leaned to the left, and a blessed breeze gave him the scent of scrub bushes and red sand. The wagon lurched, and so did his heart as his ass came off the seat, he thought he'd melded into. He grappled with one hand for the bench, pulling the reins with the other. His fingers hooked around the corner and he jerked himself back up on the bench.

Right beside a man in all black, and a black cloth over the lower half of his face.

"Hello," Doxy said, then ducked as the man took the greeting badly. He sensed the short sword skim his hair. He slapped the man across the face with the end of the reins, then wrapped the leather straps around his neck when he went down from the hit.

"Dox, down!"

His body reacted to the order, jumping off the seat and down to the floorboards.

Blood spurted around him. He looked up in just enough time to catch the body falling over him. Doxy grunted, experiencing the burn in his knee as he pushed the dead weight off him and over the side of the wagon. He grabbed the reins, astounded that the horses were still plodding along at their original pace.

Especially after witnessing Regus lift another man off his horse with his blade to hack at another, both men impaled in one swing.

"I could do that." Doxy stared in awe. The men weren't built like The Seven. They were rather slender. Starved looking. He cowered under the raised-brow-look cast at him over Regus' shoulder.

"Boy!"

Doxy twisted to see what Slayth wanted. Another all-black garbed man was stumbling toward him, weaving through the trunks and crates in the wagon's bed. "Right." He pulled his sword, impaling the man's shoulder with it. He grinned, then ended up gritting his teeth as he tried to lift him like Regus had his kill.

"One day." He told himself, pulling the sword free to stab the man again with enough force to push him off the side.

He stared at the cloud of blood behind the wagon. Within the inferno, he could see shadows of bodies flying off horses running through unharmed. A set of hooves plodded along, as if carrying the cloud. Doxy wondered what these horses had been through to not spook at this mess.

A strange rider galloped toward the wagon. Doxy stood, keeping his balance as he met them, swinging his sword into the man's face. Blood spurted, but it floated toward the cloud at the rear, as did the body.

"That was good! Take another!" Slayth's voice praised from inside the growing swirl of blood and bodies.

"Drop the reins!" Regus barked up ahead.

Doxy did as he was told, scanning for another thief. He readied himself, straightening his stance and holding his balance. Then he gritted his teeth as a sharp pain lanced through his shoulder. He looked down at the arrowhead dripping with his blood from just under his left clavicle. "So that's what that is like."

He swallowed down the bile, keeping his eyes swinging for attackers while lowering his stance so he could bob and weave unpredictably.

"Got the archer!" Regus hacked a man in half from shoulder to belly button far to the right of the wagon.

Doxy looked left in enough time to watch a woman launch herself out of the thickest clump of bushes along the roadside at him. He caught the thief with his sword, the clang of metal against metal ringing in his ears. The enemy's dagger scraped up his blade, and the singing ting of when it jumped off made Doxy twist his body and turn the edge of his sword to the woman's neck.

There wasn't much room for force, but he leaned into it with his weight and grew satisfied when the edge cut into the skin. The thief gurgled as she tumbled from the wagon. She rolled under the first wheel, thrashing, then still.

He cursed, losing his balance again and falling against the bench. The wood made the arrow push through his shoulder more, lightning shocks running from his wound outward. His fall renewed the pain in his knee. Doxy pulled himself upright, sitting with his sword at the ready as his knee throbbed and blood covered the left side of his body.

"Last one, boy!"

Doxy turned in enough time to see another climb up onto the back of the wagon. Gritting his teeth, he dropped his sword and reached under the seat to pluck the small mace out of the satchel there. He aimed, steadying himself as much as possible, taking in the roll and tumble of the wagon. He then threw with all his strength.

The sharp edges of the star mace sank into the man's throat.

"You can do better than that." Regus' voice bit into him.

Doxy grabbed another and threw it before the man could take another shuffling step toward the back of the wagon. That one hit home, right between the eyes. The spines digging in deep and cracking the skull, taking the man the rest of the way off the back of the wagon and into the swirling pool of blood.

"Good."

Doxy settled onto the bench, staring at the draft horses still walking steadily up the road as if nothing was amiss. He watched Regus riding beside him for a moment before asking, "You're witchkin, aren't you?"

"No." Regus didn't add any explanation.

"Come on! You must be! No one is that strong unless they're witchkin with strength!"

"He's not." Slayth rode up beside the wagon, the last of the blood vortex sinking into his bare hands. He chuckled, looking at Doxy with red eyes and veins protruding all over with how overfilled he was. "He's fantastic at leveraging what he has and making a show of it."

Regus grunted. "I don't make a show of things for nothing. I need fear in our enemies."

"And in your Seven, and the rest of your army," Doxy added, cringing again when Regus gave him another glare. He whimpered as his shoulder's dull ache grew tenfold with the movement.

"Let's get to the village before you bleed out." Slayth licked his lips. "You're almost still a virgin."

"Stop drinking my blood!"

Why did all of them have red hair? No, not all of them. Doxy followed the path of a blond and then a white-haired man. The woman whose eyes flashed gold as she healed him was salt and pepper haired.

Another woman kept staring at him from the corner of the healing house. She had red hair. She leaned against a wooden beam beside a large opening that let the sunlight and breeze in. The rolled canvas closure swung gently, tapping the posts it hung between. He turned, thinking that maybe it wasn't him she was staring at.

The healer grunted, smacking his cheek and then turning him back to her.

"Ouch," Doxy said softly, reaching up with his good hand to rub the slap away. Whatever drug they had given him was making him warm all over. Not an ounce of pain. Anywhere.

"He knows of our son." The woman against the post finally said.

The healer answered with another grunt.

Doxy looked between the two women. "Uh... your son?" He hoped he hadn't killed someone he wasn't supposed to. Then again, why would a member of the village harassed by the thieves be stealing from them?

"Fedvich DeLorraine Gavaintch." The healer spoke, "Son of Gachent."

"Oooh him. I want him so badly, but he doesn't care at all." Doxy groaned, falling back on the cot.

"That doesn't sound like him."

Doxy watched the healer and the other woman share a glance. "It is him! He teases and gets me hard, then goes! Poof! Gone."

He grinned as Slayth entered.

Slayth's eyes narrowed, then he sighed. "You had to give him that, grandmothers?"

"He smelled of Fedvich, blood elf."

Slayth sniffed. "How you can smell a three days' old scent has always impressed me." He eyed the healer just as she eyed him. Then added as if to sate her, "Let's call it two fools in love."

"Then we shall push Fedvich along. Send for him. Tell him the boy is near death."

"Ooooh I like her... can I hug you?" he reached for both the healer and Slayth.

Slayth shook his head. "Next time, put him to sleep."

Chapter 26: The Games of Crones

On the night of the fifth day since Doxy's departure, Fedvich's panic rose for the third time in his life. He threw things into his saddlebags. What? He wasn't sure, but he hoped it was clothing and weapons. Tossing the letter at Bertran when the man stopped him, he had to pivot away. He had to ride his horse for at least a day. After that, he could use his magic to reach Doxy quicker.

He rode into the night. Rain pelted as he pushed his horse into a gallop on the road he knew like the back of his hand. Why hadn't Regus called for him instead of Doxy? Gachent was his home. Doxy was still training. Not to mention he had a wrenched knee.

His heart thundered with his horse's hooves. Anger and fear roared in tandem in his head. What if he got there too late?

He flew off his horse at the city of Haith, tossing coins to the stable hand and slinging his stuff onto a fresh horse with long legs and a barrel chest. "I'll be back for that one, don't sell it!" Fedvich told the boy as he kicked the new one into a gallop through the double doors.

If Doxy died, he'd attack Regus. Let the man kill him. Life wasn't worth it without Doxy.

Fedvich didn't allow himself to think through his feelings. They were there. Somewhere in two years, Doxy became irreplaceable.

The next city at sunset had him sliding off the horse, taking his gear, and letting the magic swallow him whole. He burned through his reserves in three steps. His lungs and body itching with overuse, he stared across the vineyard at the log houses of his village.

One more was all he needed. He drew magic to him, grimacing as a few vines curled in on themselves before crumbling to dust. With a single step, he was in the middle of his village. Murmurs erupted among the people as they readied for the night. Scents of suppers from many of the houses wafted out of the open hangings. He waited, his jaw twitching with his tell of impatience.

Two women walked down the path, an elderly one hobbling behind them. Fedvich met them. “Grandmothers.”

“Fedvich, welcome home.” The youngest, barely gray at her temples, answered with a smile. “You’re drained. What brings you to us in such a hurry?”

“Hm, I wonder what it is, too.” The other said with a click of her tongue. “It is bad to be in such a rush.”

The eldest peered up at him, eyes bright as she grinned with most of her teeth still in. “Does he miss us?”

“Surely not us old women.” The middle-aged scoffed.

“Grandmothers,” Fedvich dropped his gear, “have you played a game?” That they weren’t rushing him to Doxy, or pointing out dangers, meant everything was well.

“We would never!”

“Far too old.” The eldest shook her head, adding an extra wobble of age to prove her point.

The youngest giggled, cupping his face in her hands and bringing him down to bump her forehead against his. “Son of us all, rid yourself of fear.” She grinned, waggling her brows. “We taught him two things. Go to him and find out what they are.”

“That is either promising and I owe you more gold than I have, or I’m in danger and I shall curse you lot for every day of my life.” He smirked when all three glared at him with smiles. “Dearest grandmothers.”

Fedvich grabbed his gear up and followed the pointing finger of the youngest grandmother. “Have supper for me, then?” He looked over his shoulder, his feet following the path down through the side of the village.

“More than your fire is warm within your house this night!”

“Don’t run. Don’t run. Walk.” He muttered, holding back so he wouldn’t make a complete fool of himself. He cursed; he was already a fool. He began a long lope, turning down a narrower path that led him further from the main houses and businesses. Everything burned within, but it didn't matter.

"Shouldn't you wash first?" She asked as she stepped into his path.

Fedvich raised a brow, stopping in front of her. "Hello, Sister."

"Brother." She shook her head at him. "He's so pale."

Fedvich grinned. "But he has the pinchable cheeks."

"Do you think he'll keep those with the wrinkles of age?"

"I hope." He bumped his forehead against hers, a hand on her shoulder. "Thank you for watching over him."

"I had to. The two with him were useless." She reached up, tapping his left shoulder. "Careful of his shoulder and his knee. You'd best bend him in half than put him on his knees, or I will kick you."

"Right. Speaking of the two..."

"Back to the port to pick up the vicious one's wife."

Fedvich couldn't believe it. "Really?"

"The bore said you had two weeks, and the blood elf told me to remind you that you owe them." She shrugged and said flippantly, "That is all."

"I already owe them my life," Fedvich admitted. "What more do they want from me?"

"Firstborn?" She grinned when Fedvich shuddered. "Oh, that's right, you're into chubby cheeks with a dick." She pushed him down the trail. "Go, I already tire of your face."

"Grow some chubby cheeks and I might like cunts again." Fedvich teased, dodging her kick to his ass by hopping into a run, ignoring the exhaustion and tightness of his body.

"I will not give my firstborn to them!" She called after him.

He chuckled, making quick work of the rest of the track. He wondered, for the hundredth time, why he wanted his house here to be at the very end of the village. The folly of an immature mind. He paused beyond the flickering light spilling from the open front flap beside his door. Fedvich sniffed himself and groaned. "I should wash."

He looked down the slope, eyeing the thin creek, then looked back at his home. "I can wash." He pushed the door open, letting his eyes adjust to fire and candlelight from the night. His home was a large room, with a smaller bath area partitioned off with canvas. His kitchen was to the right, where the fire roared in the earthen oven. A table with three chairs was in front of the kitchen. To his right was his bed.

Doxy sitting on his bed bare-chested, a sheet over his waist and legs, and hand tied to the post beside the bed was a surprise. He let his gear slip off his shoulder to land beside the entrance. "Are you a prisoner?"

"Thank the gods you're here. All I did was try to find my clothes!"

Fedvich stretched back, looking up at his ceiling and thanking the grandmothers. "Clothes are optional in Gachent."

"But I wanted mine!"

"Not an option for you, an option for the grandmothers and sisters, and Sons of Gachent."

Doxy's brows drew low. "What does that mean, exactly?"

Fedvich peeled his shirt off, tossing it over his shoulder. The washbasin was beside the bed, so he walked purposefully slow toward it, studying Doxy's face. "We helped rebuild by selling our services. They do everything else, so we are the ones who choose what goes on and doesn't here."

"Oh."

He poured the water out of the earthen container into the basin before replacing the pitcher back under the stand. He grabbed a cloth, wet it, and then added soap, lathering the cloth in his hands. Fedvich washed his face first, then his neck. He studied Doxy's wrapped shoulder as he soaped up his chest. "How bad?"

"It doesn't hurt." Doxy's voice nearly sounded like the squeak of the animals he feared.

"Hnn." Fedvich kept his smirk to himself as he sat down on the end of the bed after placing the cloth on the edge of the basin. He pulled off his boots, then stood again. Facing Doxy, he asked as he undid the buttons, "Have you eaten?"

Doxy flushed from neck to cheeks, and his eyes grew wide. The grandmothers were right to do this. Fedvich recognized his own foolishness. How could he not tell Doxy thirsted for him? He slid his pants down, tugging them off his calves and then feet. He stood again, taking the cloth and washing his back, waist, thighs, and legs. Amused how Doxy watched his hand more than anything else, he ran the soapy cloth over his half-hard cock, and then his balls.

"Doxy?"

"Fuck." Doxy blinked owlishly. "What?"

"I asked if you had eaten. Have you?"

"No." The man looked away, his free hand drawing up into his lap, wadding the sheet there. "They said they would drop it in the window after you arrived."

"They?"

"Your sister and grandmother."

Fedvich chuckled. "Not mine, but the village's." He rinsed the cloth out, then rid himself of the soap. He bent, taking the ripped cloth from his hair with a few curses at the tangles. When it was free, he dipped his head into the basin, washing his hair with the bar of soap. He then rinsed it as best he could. "But let's not talk about that right now." He stood, wringing his hair into the basin.

Fedvich tossed the wet mess back over his shoulder and put a knee on the end of the bed, getting on hands and knees to crawl toward the head, where Doxy sat. "Do you not like being naked with me?"

Chapter 27: This Is Not the Time for Questions

If Fedvich kept touching himself like that Doxy was going to spill. How embarrassing would that be? As embarrassing as three crones taking his clothes and tying him to a pole. In a bed. What bed had a pole like this? The sheets were soft, too. He had no idea of their material, but they felt like a horse's nose. All soft and velvety, but not the velvet that always came off when rubbed too hard.

That kind of velvet was horrible for a bed.

Why was he talking about food when Doxy's mouth watered for him?

Then Fedvich did that thing. That expression. It was the look that made him want to melt and hump at the same time. The one that only Fedvich could do. The countenance that made him rock hard and twitchy. Crawling. Gods fucking themselves, how could a man look that good crawling?

"Doxy?"

Again, there was a question to his name. Had he missed something other than his name? Yes. Fedvich's lips had been moving while doing that crawl with *that* look.

"I hate when you do this. You try to confuse! And you do!" Doxy cried, tilting his head back, so he was staring at the back of his eyelids.

Fedvich's chuckle made everything throb because it was different. It was dark, dangerous, like his laugh was crawling with his sex godness.

"What are you doing to me?"

"Apparently confusing you," Fedvich answered quickly.

Doxy opened his eyes and saw Fedvich was over him. Like some big cat leering over its prey, Fedvich had one hand above his on the pole, one knee beside his hip, and the other on the other side beside his thigh. He looked into the eyes and saw the green flecks glittering amid the bronze. "You are."

"What are you confused about, Doxy? I will be thrilled to clear up any misunderstandings."

His voice was like a purr, his lips so close, and Doxy could feel the heat of Fedvich's body. He swallowed, willing himself to get things straight between them before he gave in to those lips. Before he begged for the body. "I want you; do you want me?"

Fedvich's eyes flashed. "Desperately."

Did he just cum a little? Probably. Doxy's mouth watered, and he swallowed hard. "I'm not talking a one-time thing. I want you all the time. Because... because otherwise I'll be thinking about it, anyway." Fedvich's gaze dropped to his lips, his free hand came up to cup his cheek, and his thumb pressed against his bottom lip. What did that mean?

"We have two weeks of only us, then we have to go back." Fedvich's smirk was slow, "And then we will figure out a schedule of rides and training that's suitable."

Doxy groaned, "Why are you bringing Harry into this? He's the one that said that and that was when..." He replayed that day through his mind. "That was when you said you were going to fuck me that night."

"Umhm, and you turned me down, like you always do."

Fire coursed through him. "I did not! You said you weren't serious!"

The other man sighed, thumbing his lip again as if playing. "You said that it was funny. I said it wasn't. That I was serious."

Doxy was aware that his face, neck, and likely his chest, had turned red. "You said that you weren't serious."

"You have to listen for the tone, Doxy."

"Or you could just say it like you mean it!"

Fedvich chuckled and stated clearly, "Listen well, Doxy Pomm. You are mine."

"About time you gave me a straight answer, yo-" Doxy moaned into Fedvich's mouth, opening further to let his tongue slide in. He pulled at his bound limb, then gave up and used his free one to grip Fedvich's hip. He then jerked when wet droplets rained down on him, as cold as ice to his heated body. "Cold!" He pushed Fedvich's wet hair back over his shoulder while pain poked through the fading medication.

"Hmm." Fedvich's noise didn't match his wicked grin. He reached up as he asked, "Are you going to put your clothes back on?" He hooked a finger into the cord holding Doxy's wrist hostage.

"No. Never. I mean... not. No, I'm not." Doxy stared at Fedvich's hands, then looked back into the eyes that always captured him and made him bask in the glow of the redhead's attention.

"Good." With a sharp tug on one string, Fedvich freed his wrist.

"That's all it took?"

Fedvich rubbed his fingers and his palm between both hands. "Yes, love, that's all it took."

"Damnable..." Doxy pressed his lips together, then shook his head at himself. "All I could think of was you."

"Well, then, let that be the only thing on your mind." Fedvich sat back, pulling Doxy with him and on top, the sheet captured between them.

Doxy whimpered as he settled over Fedvich, straddling him. The redhead was no longer half-hard by the feel of him against his own groin. He lifted his hips a little, sliding a hand between them to do what the grandmothers suggested after they tied him up. He wrapped his hand around Fedvich's length, making sure the sheet was all around. Then he slid his hand up and down, Fedvich bucked into him.

The rubbing also did the same to his cock, and he knew the grandmother's had been right. He slid the cloth around his cock too, then lay back on Fedvich. Doxy rolled his hips, grinding against the sheet and Fedvich.

"They taught you one thing at least," Fedvich panted, his hands cupping Doxy's ass and squeezing.

Doxy moaned, then hissed as the pressure built up and made his half-healed shoulder and knee ache.

"That won't do." Fedvich murmured, rolling them to their sides. He pulled Doxy's thigh up over his before placing his hand back on the rounded ass cheek. "Better?"

Doxy nodded. The friction was delicious, almost like he was in someone.

Fedvich leaned, rolling Doxy half to his back to put more pressure on them. He rocked his hips in a slow roll, hand gripping the pale globe of his lover's ass cheek. He propped up on his elbow, looking down at Doxy as he worked him.

Doxy huffed, looking between them at how Fedvich's body moved, then back up to his mouth. The bastard looked like he could do this all day, had done it all day. So relaxed and not at all driven wild. Except for the flash of his eyes, the way his jaw was tight. This close, Doxy could see the tension. He drove his fingers into Fedvich's tangled, wet hair, dragging the man's mouth to his.

Fedvich's thrusts grew harder as their tongues rubbed against one another.

They parted, panting, thrusting hard and fast. Doxy bit his bottom lip, trying to last. Desperate for Fedvich to cum, to see what that looked like on his facc, hc ground harder.

Then Fedvich said against his lips before kissing him, "Let go."

It was as if following orders was so ingrained that his body did as it was told. He jerked several times before his body pulled taut. His release hit him hard. His moan caught by Fedvich's mouth, his seed spilling into the wondrous sheet made for fucking because, of course, it was.

"Fedvich?"

"Hn?" The redhead smiled down at him.

"You're still hard."

Fedvich chuckled. "By some luck, yes, that I am."

"I want to see your face when you lose it."

Fedvich's eyes flickered again, hunger filling them along with the glimmering green sparks. "Doxy, you never have to fear I won't spill for you. It took all my willpower to not do so then."

"But why not?" Doxy still hadn't caught his breath, but he wanted to make Fedvich just as relaxed as him first.

"Because I'm going to keep you up well into the morning hours to see if you beg me to stop or if you're just as fucked as I am in needing you."

"Oh, I am fucked." Doxy realized what it meant. He understood Fedvich's level of skill, how much more of a professional he was in that moment.

"Not yet, but you are," Fedvich said with a chuckle.

Chapter 28: Bigger Blacker Cave

"Does your knee hurt?" Fedvich asked through huffed breaths, pulling Doxy's hips back to him so he could sink in deep, then helping him pull away with a gentle push.

"Stop asking. Keep fucking." Doxy said, both hands wrapped around the pole, with arms flexing with every push and pull of their thrusts.

Fedvich experienced the thrill of hearing Doxy's voice while hard and inside all over again. This man could keep up with him. He couldn't get enough. His eyes dropped to Doxy's ass cheeks jiggling with each hit of his hips, and he whimpered.

He always made that mistake. Why did they look so good doing that around his cock? How did this kind of magic work where everything the man did both aroused him more and made him want to cum at the same instant?

Whatever it was, he could figure it out later. He couldn't think. Didn't want to. He gripped Doxy's hips harder, driving into him with all the force he could muster. Triumph crawled over him as Doxy threw back his head to cry out with each thrust, a few of those cries his name.

His lover was indeed dramatic. Loud when reaching the cliff's edge and screaming over it. But this loud, dramatic man, a one Doxy Pomm, was his to fuck anytime he wanted.

Two more rough, slapping thrusts and Doxy shuddered around him, seed plopping to the floor. Fedvich wasn't far behind. He rode his orgasm out inside Doxy, holding them flush together as he pumped everything he had left in him out. Sliding out, he turned his lover to face him before pressing him up against the pole. He fit his mouth against the other, tasting him deeply before releasing. "Rest while I see what our breakfast is."

He waited until Doxy was crawling up on the bed, because that sight would never get old, before going to the window that acted like a drop-off. He picked up the basket, plucking out a flaky bread and taking a bite. "Mmm, grandmothers blessed us. We don't have to suffer through sister's burnt fare."

"Was that the twentieth?"

Fedvich smiled around his next bite, pausing in his approach to the bed to watch Doxy's glistening chest rise and fall. "I no longer fancy counting how many times I make my partners orgasm."

"What's the most you've done?"

Fedvich sat down beside his lover, crossing his legs as he faced him, setting the basket of biscuits, dried meat, cheeses, and jams at Doxy's side. "With a single, or do you wish me to count the orgies?"

He chuckled when Doxy groaned, covering that rounded-cheeked face with his hands. "I'm supposed to be the best anyone has ever had, love. Don't worry yourself over my past."

"I'm not. I mean... I don't want to bore you."

Fedvich stilled, staring down at his lover, who kept his gaze averted. He sighed, tossing his half-eaten biscuit back into the basket. He got up on his hands and knees, straddling the man who held his heart before pulling Doxy's hands away from his face. Leaning down, he pinned Doxy's wrists to the bed, careful with his wounded arm. "If I am bored, I assure you it will never be your fault. We have plenty to explore together, trust me. Even if you are satisfied with doing what we've just done for the rest of our lives, that will thrill me because it's you."

Doxy's mouth worked before he said, "I'm not like Harry, or Regus, or Slayth, or-"

"If you say Bertran, no one touches Bertran, not even Bertran himself. And I've only had Charn in my mouth." Fedvich shook his head. "No, you are not those. Harry was my best student and friend – still is, I served Regus if he needed some release, I have never touched Slayth. But you, Doxy, you are the one who stood there on your first day and made me desire you. No one has ever done that. No one has ever kept me enthralled for longer than a day. You've had my interest for two years."

"I have? How?"

Fedvich chuckled, "If I knew that, then I would have figured out how to fuck you before two-gods-forsaken-years of torment kept me from you."

The men talked between bites, and sometimes around them. Fedvich watched Doxy polish off his last two mouthfuls as he asked, "Ready to see the village? I want to show you something."

"I still don't have my clothes."

"Naked is preferable."

"It is not!" Doxy's face bloomed red.

Fedvich laughed. "Very well, my shy lover." He swung his feet to the floor and stood. He took a moment to stretch. He was sorer than he cared to admit, but he'd be damned if he let it ruin this day. Walking over to a small dresser in the corner, to open the first drawer. He dug through it, frowning when he didn't find what he wanted. The third drawer proved fruitful at last. "Here." He straightened, striding over to hold up a swath of cloth for Doxy to study.

"What is that?" Doxy eyed it more like it was going to eat him than clothe him.

"A traditional cover." Fedvich watched Doxy's face closely.

"Cover for what?! My arm? Where's the rest of it?"

Fedvich held back the laugh with a cough. "This is it. Stand up, I'll put it on you." He enjoyed how Doxy did as he was told, so docile at times. He wrapped the cloth around Doxy's hips, tying it and adjusting the angle. "Perfect." Doxy's ass was made for the short wrap, barely hidden, and such easy access. It showed off the thick thighs, too.

"That's it?" Doxy twisted, looking down at himself. He ran a hand over the fabric, his neck, ears, and face getting redder by the second. "This is not it."

"It is, and it suits you." Fedvich took the other wrap he'd pulled off his shoulder. He situated it around his waist, swiftly tying it in place.

"Why can't I have that?! Trade!" Doxy fumbled the knot at his hip.

Fedvich chuckled, the heavy fabric hanging to his ankles. He adjusted the adornment to the front; a flexible cloth made with shining threads that was in stark contrast to the black of the skirt. He smacked Doxy's hands away when the boy was about to figure out the knot.

Doxy's face nearly purpled as he stared and pointed. "Why is that the same size as your hard cock?"

"Advertisement."

Doxy whimpered, covering his face with his hands.

Fedvich couldn't help but laugh again as he grabbed the comb from beside the washbasin. He ran it through Doxy's hair a few times, the dirty blond strands were so soft the tangles released easily. It had been a while since he treated his hair as he should. He grimaced as the comb caught more times than he liked through his own tresses.

"Shouldn't we wash off?"

"No, I'm going to show you a proper bath."

Doxy nodded. "Right, either way, I'm naked."

"If it was up to me, you would remain naked for my pleasure at all times." Fedvich smirked, finishing with his hair and replacing the comb. He grabbed Doxy's hand, "Come." He tugged the younger man behind him. No one dared stop them, but oh, did most want to.

Fedvich's pride soared as he noted the eyes on his lover as they strode down the path until it forked. He took the higher one, heading toward the gently rolling mountains behind the village. He turned, watching as they drooled over how Doxy's ass looked in the skirt, even with the limp. A peek was all they would get, and Fedvich wanted them to know it. Doxy was his. He would get what he was owed for the two years of torture. The trail turned up, then down as it curved into the mountain. Torches covered the walls, lighting the path as if the sun shone in toward the end of the tunnel. He pulled Doxy to his side, walking beside him. He kept his gaze on his lover as the chamber opened.

The walls were black as night; a few gray stripes and speckles cut through the polished stone. The carvers shaped the chamber so that the tunnel and the wall directly across formed the closest point of the cavern. In the center of those points was a tall, narrow spire jutting toward the ceiling. White veins of a unique stone crackled through it, lending an eerie light until they joined at the bulbous white head. The rounded head was the light source in the room as it glowed and pulled the sun's rays to disperse them throughout.

Doxy didn't disappoint. His mouth hung open in awe as he stared at the phallus jutting from the clear water. Then those thick brows drew together as his eyes darted around, taking in the rest of the room. Fedvich bit back a grin as Doxy's blush returned.

"This honors the Sons of Gachent."

"Of course it does."

Fedvich shook hard in his laughter.

"Are we bathing here? in the balls?"

"No, my love, this particular manhood is sacred. The baths are this way." Fedvich guided him along the edge of the pool to the left. He stepped into the entrance, hidden from view by clever carvers. Down this tunnel, he let go of Doxy's hand and placed it on his lovcr's lower back.

Damp heat grew with each step. Then they entered the next chamber, split into two by a thick wall of the same black and gray stone. The glowing white stone was all around, even underneath the water that filled the chamber. The water was milky and steaming. Few were in the chambers, those that were took one glance at the new arrivals and then ignored them.

Fedvich let Doxy take it all in before taking the man's wrap off. He untied his own, letting it fall to the dry floor. "It's hot, so let yourself adjust." He murmured, standing directly behind Doxy and urged him with a gentle nudge of his hips.

Chapter 29: The First Son of Gachent

Year of Survival of Bertran Training, 24 years ago, less one night and a tyrant

None of the others were hurt, and Fedvich cursed himself. Slayth examined him, pulling his leather shirt up and prodding at the slice over his ribs. "Nothing broke."

"Genius," Fedvich muttered, then played dumb; trying his sweetest smile and batting his eyelashes at the elder.

Slayth pulled a swath of white cotton out of the small pack Bertran carried on his left thigh. He pressed it across the cut. "Hold." Fedvich did as he was told, then hissed as Slayth's quick movements wrapped the cloth around him and pulled his ribs together. "I don't need a corset."

"But it brings out your figure." Slayth mimicked Fedvich's voice rather poorly before ripping the cloth with his teeth and tying it off with the other end.

"You girls done? We have a king's army to kill."

Fedvich glared up at Bertran. He definitely hated the man more than he liked him. "With five?"

"Four, you two little ones barely count as half each." Bertran again.

"Don't." Fedvich shook his head at Harry when the redhead snorted. Of course, the prince didn't listen.

Harry pointed at the old man with his whip. "Here I thought you were counting yourself as half, and the blood elf the other, considering your ages."

The grins the old males sported made Fedvich shiver from head to toe.

"Tell you what, Prince," Slayth began, tucking the roll of cloth back in Bertran's bag. "If you kill more than any of the rest of us, I'll give you a prize."

"What's the prize?"

"You and your lover there get two days off after this."

Harry frowned, "That's hardly anything."

"Take it!" Fedvich hissed, launching himself close enough to grab Harry's arm. "Days off are better than a bag of gold."

"Two days off *and* a bag of gold each."

Slayth chuckled. "Done."

Regus stood, swinging his sword to stretch each of his arms out. "I suppose we should begin."

The men trickled out of the room. Fedvich held Harry back with him to take up the rear. "Do you realize what you just did?"

Harry lifted a shoulder. "Killed a king, his royal guard, and made a bet with old men?"

"Besides that, you announced you were going to kill at least a third of the army waiting for us."

Harry laughed. "A third? I'll only have to kill fifty at best."

Fedvich groaned and pinched the bridge of his nose. "I swear if I have to start training over again because of your mouth, I'll cut your tongue out."

"You'll miss it more than me."

He canted his head to the side, thinking of the things he taught Harry, then sighed. "Right." He thought of another punishment: "I'll keep my tongue from you."

Harry stopped walking, his eyes slightly wider than normal. He cleared his throat, "A third, you said?"

"A third."

As they spoke, the men before them peeled off to the side, letting them go in front. "Fuck. Fuck. Fuck." Fedvich muttered to himself, pulling his sword off his back after unsheathing a dagger. Two weapons, double the kills. Right? He hoped. Fedvich put his back to the wall before the wide opening that was the staircase leading down to the largest room of the castle, the foyer formerly used as a ballroom. He peered around the corner, cursing when he had to jerk back as arrows thunked into the wall beside his head.

“Any day now,” Regus said dryly behind him.

Fedvich muttered more curses under his breath, trying to think of how he should do this.

He took too long.

The baron, in two long strides, put his hand on the banister and leaped over it in one graceful move that Fedvich admired before he realized Regus would be dead before his feet hit the floor. He rushed forward in time to see arrows bouncing off the broadsword Regus held in front of him. The lord’s feet hit, the sword slashed in a half-moon through the air, followed by crunching bones and the spurt of blood.

Not witchkin. A god, Fedvich thought to himself before falling back as pain ripped through his arm. He cursed, breaking off the shaft of the arrow. He was thankful the head came out the other side. He watched Harry step over him, whips in each hand, lashing out, followed by screams. His lover walked down that staircase as if he were debuting at a ball. Well, with whips and screams and blood and...

“Can’t you get through one room without being wounded, boy?” Slayth glared as he placed a large hand on his shoulder. The elder elf yanked out the arrow. Then he moved on, guards running up the stairs turned pale before blood erupted from their mouths and eyes and flowed toward Slayth like strings.

He started up, then Bertran was on him, wrapping more bandage around him, tying a tight knot over the wound in his arm. “Next time, use that speed, create a diversion. Form up.”

Fedvich followed Harry, Slayth and Bertran down the stairs, thankful he still had his dominant hand and sword. The dagger’s weight hurt, but he hoped he could manage. Regus swung again, two soldiers flying up to smack against the wall above his head wetly. He didn’t take the time to watch them fall to the floor.

Regus had cleared a path to the bottom of the stairs and took his position. His sword swung from side to side, then arced up, then back to the right. The crunch of metal, the screams of men, the thunder of boots on stone was deafening. Slayth and Bertran were behind Regus, fanned out like a wide-based triangle to give Regus plenty of room to swing and move.

Fedvich made the end of the diamond shape, taking care of any leftovers or those that circled around behind the men up front. Harry waded to the middle of the room, driving the enemy to them with whiplashes that popped faster than Fedvich could count.

"Damn that boy," Slayth hissed, pulling the blood out of one soldier and drowning another with it, only to repeat the process.

"What?" Bertran asked, glancing back for a second before smashing the heads of two soldiers together, crushing them with a sickening wet crunch.

"He's driving them to us."

"And?"

"What we kill are his kills, too."

Fedvich grinned, "Told you you would like him."

"*Like* is such a strong word." Regus growled, carving a path out of the ranks, filling the ballroom from the open double doors ahead.

Each step he took, they followed. Fedvich, for the third time, marveled at the number of bodies behind them. "Why do I doubt you three couldn't kill an entire army?"

"Four, now five, boy."

Regus roared, the two eldest shoved Fedvich forward into Regus' position, and pulled Regus to the back. Two blades stuck out from the baron, one in his right shoulder and one in his left thigh. Fedvich sheathed his other dagger and began swinging his sword with both hands in swaths, making sure to twist slightly up or down to gain access to the neck or bellies. He was doing it. He was holding the formation. Pride entered Fedvich, even as pain attempted to make him surrender.

Then Regus was beside him. "Back into formation."

Fedvich stared, taking a step back. The blades were broken, the metal barely sticking out of Regus' body. He glanced over to Bertran, the old man was dripping with sweat and huffing.

"I'm exceedingly glad that I am not your enemy." Harry yelled over the din, "Never thought I'd see anyone break swords."

Had Bertran broken them? With his bare hands? Fedvich shook his head, focusing on the task at hand as he took up his spot at the rear again. He angled his head, observing Regus's swing. He noted its diminished speed. Perhaps he was half-god?

Then Regus went down on one knee, his growling war cry echoing through the chamber over the screams.

Fedvich turned, ready to take the head position back again, when he noticed there were men fleeing from the doors, trying to give them a wide berth as they kept running. He started to follow, to kill those cowards, but Slayth put a hand on his shoulder.

"Not our problem anymore, boy."

Fedvich shook his head. "How is it..." Three men in silver armor entered, swords bloodied, then one in white armor with a blood-red cape. Slayth and Bertran dipped to one knee on each side of Regus. Fedvich hurried to do the same.

"I must say, I wasn't expecting to have such little resistance when taking a country." The king's voice rang out, youthful and jubilant. "I commend you, baron. Or shall I say... duke. Yes, Duke Regus Norvasos, this victory is all thanks to you." Fedvich stared as the king touched Regus' shoulders with his bare hands, then placed fingertips on the baron's forehead as he spoke. The king then turned. "Healers!"

"Ah, payment." The king stated with a smile as the healers scurried in, took one glance at Regus, gasped, and quickly began their work. With a flick of his wrist, five men came in, carrying two black sacks each, all nearly scraping the ground with their thick bottoms.

The sacks clanked when the group sat them down in front of the five of them. Fedvich stared into the slight opening of one of his, his breath catching at the shining gold coins within. "This is how I will rebuild the village."

"Son, this is how you can rebuild ten." Slayth chuckled, pounding his back.

Chapter 30: Took You Long Enough

Two weeks were not long enough. Would they die if they resigned? He wouldn't mind living in the village. He might get used to being naked all the time.

Doubt crept up through his thoughts. What if, when they got back, Fedvich began his old lifestyle again? Teaching others, being a whore in a way, and how would they handle that? Would he be happy that Fedvich came back to him? Or would Fedvich stay with him?

He turned to stare at Fedvich, half-dressed in their uniform. Pants on, shirt wide open and untucked, feet bare, the man was sexy without trying. He always was. Doxy tried to imagine Fedvich a little over twenty years ago. When the man rode in and dropped a bag of gold at the grandmothers' feet. How did that victorious action appear on the sculpted features?

"You keep staring at me like that and I'll ride you all the way back." Fedvich said, jerking the strings into a knot on his saddlebags.

Doxy's face flamed as if he'd just lit a fire in front of himself. "The horses on the wagon would probably follow the road without guidance." He stared at Fedvich, wondering where that had come from. Had he really said that out loud?

There was that sex-god look on his lover's pretty face, making it utterly sinful. Hunger. That made him rock hard if he didn't think of something gross or painful.

"Stop it!"

"You're the one suggesting to fuck in a wagon for three days, or four." Fedvich's desire was in his voice.

Doxy cursed, realizing he was lost and would walk through the village half-hard. Then the worst thing happened.

The three grandmothers, and the one Fedvich called 'sister,' entered. Didn't they knock or wait to be told all was clear?

Of course not. Why would they when their menfolk all walked around naked and half the time they were too? The eldest hobbled to him, and Doxy wished her face was enough to make him soft again. But his lover was still in the room, and his body was bolder than his head.

Fedvich stood beside him. "Grandmothers?"

She smiled, leaning her cane against the bed where Doxy packed his bag. She reached up, cupping their cheeks, then she held on to Fedvich's. "Son of Gachent no more. You are Father now, for your loyalty in love shall provide inspiration to us all."

Fedvich grinned, kissing her palms. "Thank you, grandmother."

"And you," she said, turning to Doxy, and a gnarled finger made his eyes cross, "You are young, he is old, make sure he drinks plenty of water to keep up with you."

Doxy strangled on his own saliva and his whole body heated. "I-"

"I'm not old," Fedvich countered before Doxy could get anything out. "I'm still in my prime."

The grandmother reached behind the men, grabbing her cane as she laughed and said, "You are no daisy."

Fedvich huffed. "Daisies don't last as long as I have. I'm of better stock."

Doxy's mind whirled. "Wait, he doesn't have to sell himself for the village anymore?"

"He didn't have to from the beginning, he chose to. Sons are not forced, and he was the first one to do such a grand gesture, anyway." The sister answered from behind the grandmothers, the closest to the door as if she needed a quick escape.

"The biggest bag of gold, but not the biggest dick." The middle grandmother teased. "Of which we are grateful."

The youngest grandmother made a face. "There is a reason why the biggest son did not make as much as this son, he scared many."

Cool hands covered his burning ears before Fedvich said, "Don't talk about the bigger one of my master's, he's a curious sort and I will not have him sate it."

"I wouldn't!" Doxy cried, then groaned as the lot of them laughed. Why was he always walking straight into being the butt of a joke?

"My ass hurts." Doxy groaned after getting off the wagon.

"I can fix that." A waggle of his brows accompanied Fedvich's grin as he jumped off to stand beside him.

His face flushed, and he pressed his back against the wagon. "Someone will see!" He whimpered when Fedvich leaned on a hand placed beside his shoulder, the other slid around to pull him off the wagon and flush to the other man's body.

"While using that excuse before I witnessed how voracious you were worked, it does not now."

"It should work more!" Doxy pushed against Fedvich's chest. Not with his full strength, no, because Fedvich's hand was now on his ass and kneading the soreness out of it. Why wouldn't he want that? "You know how I get when you touch me."

"Why, yes, I certainly do. I know how you *get* me to touch you."

Fedvich's lips brushed the shell of his ear. He couldn't help but glance around to see if anyone was watching. "I don't do anything."

"No. Not anything at all."

That familiar tone when Fedvich said things he didn't mean was blatant these days. It hadn't been at all before, and Doxy blamed himself for all those missed opportunities. What if he could surprise the man, always turning him on?

Doxy pressed into Fedvich, sliding his hands down over the man's sides to rest them on the narrow hips before him.

When Fedvich pulled back to peer at him, Doxy kissed him. He trailed the tip of his tongue along Fedvich's bottom lip until he opened to him. He drew the kiss in deeper.

Fedvich pressed his full body against Doxy, trapping him against the wagon.

A sound came from the redhead, then another. Doxy wondered if he was about to be stripped down and taken out in the open against the wagon. The idea made him twitch in multiple places, but he kept on kissing his lover.

His lover. Fedvich. The best-looking, most aggravating man he knew was his. The sex god was even grinding into him and making little whimpering noises as if his need for him was too much.

"About time."

Doxy froze.

"Took them long enough. Had to listen to both whining for what? three years? four?"

"Two, damn you." Fedvich growled, pulling away from Doxy and turning to glare. "Two was more than enough!" Then the redhead froze for a moment, before turning to study Doxy's face.

Doxy stared up into the metallic eyes he loved, watching the green glimmer in them. "What?"

"You whined to them about me?"

Doxy flushed. "Well, I didn't- couldn't- they listened and I wouldn't call it whining really, just talking to them and get-" He moaned into Fedvich's mouth as the other man kissed him hungrily.

"That's what I like to see. He's still got it. No more flaccid cocks for him."

Doxy pulled away, looking behind Fedvich to the grinning redhead who then gave him a wink, then back to Fedvich who was currently licking his neck then... "Oh!" He arched, then cursed, the pinch of teeth sinking into his neck, and then the hard suck.

"Don't have to mark him, boy. We know he's off-limits. Has been since you saw his little shy grin thing he does." Slayth said, then shook his head and began walking toward the main house.

The sun added an orange glow to the blue sky waning into darkness. His stomach gave a growl as Fedvich squeezed his ass in both hands. Doxy hissed, grabbing handfuls of Fedvich's hair and pulling his mouth off his neck with a pop that sounded most satisfying, but now wasn't the time to ruminate on that. "We're being watched and teased!"

Fedvich raised his eyebrows. "Love, we're always being watched and teased here, what difference does it make if I'm kissing you or standing dumbfounded beside you?"

Doxy started to say something, but there wasn't really anything to say. Fedvich was right. He sighed, slumping back against the wagon. "Can we keep our fucking from prying eyes at least?"

Harry huffed, "That was going to be the best part. I have yet to see a Pomm fully flush. Addy doesn't blush anymore. At all. Gods, she made *me* blush the other day."

Fedvich chuckled. "That's a feat, well done, Adeline."

Doxy groaned as the two men turned as if Fedvich hadn't been about to fuck him in broad daylight. He couldn't figure out what was worse: not knowing Fedvich's emotions or knowing and still having to temper his drive.

Chapter 31: Creatures of the Night, What Music They Make

First it was being brought up to Regus' office, which he hardly visited. Then this declaration. He hadn't heard right. "What?"

"You and Doxy can live here until you find a house of your own," Regus said then took a sip of his blood-red wine.

"But... why? The barracks..."

"Need their sleep, not jacking off while listening to you two all night long."

That made sense. "Here?"

Regus' brow twitched. "Are you going to make me repeat every word multiple times, or are you going to use your brain at some point during this conversation?"

Fedvich bit the inside of his cheek to keep from saying what he wanted to. He thought through some options and finally landed on something civil. "It's strange that you're opening your house to me after having Harry live here. We've known each other for a long while, and you have never made an offer like this."

"You've never been in love."

Fedvich stared at Regus, then he chuckled. "That woman has made you soft."

"Fine, live in the creek."

"No! I appreciate the offer, and I will move into Doxy's rooms here tonight!" Fedvich held up a hand, then had to laugh again. "What about you? Will you rest, or will you and your wife listen?"

Regus raised a brow as he said, "Be wary of what you wish for, my lady makes beautiful sounds."

"I would think so." Fedvich chuckled. "I remember making all the sounds when you pounded into me, too."

"I am aware Harry gave her some tips, but you haven't taught her anything, have you?"

Fedvich shook his head, wondering where Regus was going with this again. "No, not at all. I didn't want to charm her away from you, and Harry was a safer tutor."

Regus snorted, "I appreciate that."

He watched his duke and commander drink down the wine. "Do you believe her yet?"

"On what?"

"When she tells you she loves you and that you're handsome?" When Regus rolled his eyes, Fedvich had his answer. Damn the old men for convincing Regus he was ugly, so they wouldn't have so much work chasing women away. One day, Regus would know what he was worth, and Fedvich hoped he'd still be alive to see it. "So... any secrets you want to tell me... like being a god or witchkin or something?"

"You're still on about that?"

"Of course I'm still on about that! Look at you! Gorgeous, and then you go and can throw ten men off a sword without breaking a sweat." Fedvich stopped when Regus smirked.

"My sword isn't long enough to hold ten men on it."

"That's what you want to focus on?" Fedvich sighed, leaning his head against the back of the couch. "Have I thanked you for giving me this life?"

"No. You've cursed me. Hundreds of times."

Fedvich chuckled, regarding Regus through half-lidded eyes. "Thank you, brother."

Regus grumbled, "You're welcome."

Fedvich jumped up. "Give me a hug."

"No." Regus sprang up as well, keeping the desk and second couch between them. "Back!"

Fedvich made his bottom lip tremble and widened his eyes. "All I want is a little hug from you because we were having a moment and you tell me to get back like I'm some filthy beast!"

"Regus! Give Fedvich a hug!"

Regus cringed, seeing his wife in the doorway.

Fedvich kept up the pout, making his lip tremble harder and his eyes water when Regus focused on him again. The act grew more difficult when Regus took a few steps forward. Then he looked into the dark as night eyes and saw murder. He held up his hands, backing away a step.

"What? Don't want the hug anymore?"

"Not when you have that look!" Fedvich cried, panic clawing at his throat. He feinted to the right, then ran left. He grunted when something hard hit his stomach and lifted him off his feet. "God. I swear, you're a god." He fought for air when he was brought to his lord's broad chest and that other arm gripped him. "Ribs! My ribs!"

"Regus!"

Fedvich fell to the floor, gasping for breath. He glared up at Regus, who was grinning with his hands in the air. He groaned, rolling onto his back and splaying out. "I had flashbacks. Terrible ones."

"Of what?" Virsin's sweet voice reached him from somewhere behind the beast of a man.

"Of me not being able to walk for three days."

Regus chuckled. "You offered to relieve the pressure."

"Only because I feared what you would do to the women!" Fedvich pointed up at him. "You'd crush them in one hand!" He stared at the little, dainty hand on Regus' arm, then smiled up at Virsin who stared down at him with pursed lips.

"He's a very giving, gentle lover." Virsin stated with a sly smirk.

"If I had known I was going to be lied to tonight, I would have drunk more." He rolled his eyes.

"If he needs to have such roughness now and then, I'm sure Doxy won't mind sharing you."

Fedvich rolled to his feet and gave the couple a wide berth as he strode toward the door. "No, Doxy's the jealous type. Never wants me out of his sight. Speaking of! I should go find him."

He shuddered as he took the stairs two at a time down to the dining room. The last time Regus had him, he had handprints on his hips for weeks, among other pains. Fedvich followed the sounds of laughter and Doxy's adamant, flustering speeches to the dining room.

"I do not need to wear a maid's uniform!"

"Oh, please, Doxy, you will be so cute!"

Fedvich leaned against the doorframe, watching Addy plead with her brother. He caught Harry's eyes and tilted his head. The other redhead winked.

"One with a short skirt, Fedvich adores your ass. All you'd have to do is bend over slightly to show off those bloomers and he'll jump you like he's never had you before." Harry claimed, his eyes still on Fedvich.

He couldn't deny it. Seeing Doxy in a maid outfit would be comical, and fucking him in it would be divine.

"See!" Addy bounced in her seat at Harry's side, across the table from Doxy.

Charn groaned. "Just put on the dress and be done with it already."

"No!" Doxy cried, then slumped in his chair as the men teased him more about how good he would be with high-heeled boots on, too. "Besides, if I wore one, none of you would know. Only him."

Fedvich nearly melted. How sweet his Doxy was. He stalked forward, catching Addy's eyes and shaking his head at her. Bertran wouldn't give him away, the man's face was always stone. He leaned over Doxy's chair, whispering in his lover's ear, "Want me to dress in one first?"

He saw the full body tremble and the goosebumps on his lover's neck. Had Doxy already been picturing him in one? He had to ask later.

"No!" Not that... maybe? Yes. I think that would be good. I'd... we... can we..." Doxy whimpered, covering his face with his hand while the other still gripped the arm of the chair like it was a lifeline.

Fedvich chuckled, kissing Doxy's cheek. "Come along, my Pomm, we have things to gather."

"So, you are living here? With us?" Addy was bouncing in that seat again, and Fedvich wondered if that was how she rode Harry.

"Yes. For now."

Doxy shot up, turning to stare at Fedvich with wide eyes. "We can't!"

"It's basically an order, Dox." Fedvich took his hand and led him out of the dining room. He heard Charn become the next victim of teasing. "Regus doesn't want us to keep the barracks up at night any longer."

He watched Doxy's pale face turn into a similar shade as a tomato. He bit back a laugh, opening the door for Doxy as the servants were too busy dealing with the raucous diners. "Never fear, love, once we get our own place, you can scream my name until you can no longer."

Chapter 32: From the First Time I Laid Eyes on You, I Was Yours

Decades of Survival of Bertran Training, 2 years ago, trainee introduction day...

"How many did we get this time?"

"Ten."

"That's low."

Fedvich shook his head. "We're not at war anymore. There's no money in being here."

Harry yawned, stretching before leaning against the wall beside Fedvich. "Honor, kids are all about honor these days."

"Honor, power, money — it's all the same." Fedvich lifted a shoulder, watching their soldiers march into formation. "I still find it odd that we have six."

"Six is still all we need; the rest are just to keep up appearances." Harry laughed, "No, one is all we need, the rest of us are there to pick off the strays."

"Did you see the latest letter from our king?" Fedvich grinned, leaning toward Harry. When the other redhead shook his head in denial, he added, "He wants Regus to marry."

Harry snorted, "Not a chance. Slayth and Bertran made sure he'd never think himself good enough for a lady. He hardly touches whores."

"That might be a good thing in some cases." Fedvich muttered, remembering the finger-shaped bruises. It both scared him and made him salivate, because he knew he was the only one who handled Regus well. "Could you imagine what she would be like? His ideal?"

Harry tilted his head to the side.

It had been a while since Harry thought of such things. It wasn't Harry's job to teach pleasure, or to give it, so he didn't need to figure out what would gain him the most coin and the fastest orgasm out of a client. Fedvich practiced it often and well. "She'd have to have a bit to her. He cannot go for any of the proper ladies we see around the king."

"No," Harry agreed. "Think he might be a blonde guy?"

"Yeah, none of us closest to him are blond, so he wouldn't be traumatized by it." Fedvich chuckled and shook his head. "Definitely cannot be an elf."

Harry shuddered. "No, any part of Regus that would live forever would be too long."

Fedvich and Harry's conversation trailed off as Regus left the barracks. On his heels, in single file line were the new recruits. Little lords or members of the lower class who wanted to touch the fame that was The Six. They recruited twice a year, and each year the numbers dwindled. Slayth and Bertran trailed the newcomers, standing behind them as they faced the army before them.

Fedvich nodded to Charn, who stood across the expanse of the training field. Then he focused on the new boys. Each year the numbers were sorry, and their faces looked more haggard. Except for one.

One stood in the middle, shorter than the rest, better dressed than the rest of them, too. His face was round, cheeks looking as soft as peaches. Needing discipline to stay out of his eyes, the mop of blond hair was browner at the roots than at the tips.

The first boy introduced himself, and Fedvich didn't hear a word. This is also true for the second, third, and fourth. On the fifth, he only heard that trembling voice. "I'm Doxy Pomm, second son of Viscount Pomm, pleasure to meet you, and I hope to be of service." The boy laughed nervously, hand rubbing the back of his neck.

Those cheeks blushed red.

He jumped at the sharp elbow to his ribs.

"Ooooh you got it bad." Harry crooned, his grin aggravatingly wide.

"Got what bad? I have no idea what you're talking about." He returned his gaze to Doxy Pomm, unable to stay away.

"The love or immediate lust. I'm never sure which with you, but it's usually lust. It was love with me, and I've only seen that once."

Fedvich snorted. "I didn't love you at first sight."

Harry sighed, wrapping an arm around his shoulders and leaning heavily. "Oh, I understand. You adore me. Dream about me. Can't wait for me to enter the room. But that little one in the middle, I can see how you want him. He'll replace me in your dreams tonight, I'm sure."

Fedvich tried to shrug off Harry's arm, muttering as he couldn't. "I do love you, adore you, dream of you, but I can have you anytime I want."

"So it's the chase."

Fedvich glared, finally tearing his eyes away from the rosy-cheeked Pomm. "Do you comprehend the meaning behind the words that are coming out of your mouth, or are you just spouting nonsense? There is no chase. There is no dreaming of a young man tonight either."

"He's probably thirteen, tops." Harry said, studying the Pomm boy.

Fedvich rolled his eyes. "Wc can't sign them unless they're fourteen. He's nineteen."

"You're going blind in your old age. I thought sex was supposed to be good for the eyes."

"It is, and I'm not. I can see perfectly well. You've never been a good judge of age, nor character."

"We'll just have to see. Our turn." Harry strode forward.

Fedvich cursed. "No, don't you dare!"

Harry lengthened his stride into a slow lope, glancing at Fedvich over his shoulder with another irritating grin.

Fedvich shot forward, grabbing Harry's hair and yanking back. Harry let out a sound that could have been in a house of ill repute before falling on his backside. He glared, trying to jerk his hair out of Fedvich's hand by pulling with both of his. Fedvich smirked, flinging down the ends, so they smacked solid against Harry's chest. He loped toward the stage as the man begged for more.

He glanced down at his hand, tsking at the sight of pinpricks of blood appearing. "Welcome, fresh blood," Fedvich said with his winning smile and kept it up since Slayth and Bertran loudly groaned. His gaze swept down the line, watching some hands cover their fronts. He loved this part of the job.

Except Pomm didn't seem to react. At all. What was that all about?

So distracted, or distraught he wasn't sure which, he forgot to monitor Harry's approach.

"Well, well, we have some fine recruits." Harry purred, sauntering over to the middle. "Especially you, chipmunk. How old are you?"

Fedvich inwardly groaned, but he couldn't take his eyes off the kid as those cheeks filled with red color again.

"It's Doxy Pomm, sir. I'm twenty-eight."

Was the ground still there, or was he flying? Fedvich glanced around, noting the shock on more faces than what might be on his. Twenty-eight?

"You don't have to lie; you're already signed on. You're thirteen, aren't you?"

Sometimes Harry had tact, and there were most times where he didn't. This was one of those untactful times, obviously. Fedvich kicked him in the shin. But Harry ignored it, peering into the baby-faced recruit too close for comfort.

The red seemed to change hues. The Pomm's brown eyes shot daggers as the boy drew up to his full height. "I assure you, sir, that I am twenty-eight. I'm the second-born son of Viscount Pomm with two brothers and a sister younger than me, also in their twenties. I shouldn't need to prove this to you."

Harry whistled low, straightening and rocking back on his heels. "What do you think, Fedvich? Still want to fuck him even though he's twenty-eight?"

Fedvich smiled sweetly. "I want to fuck those willing." Inwardly, he cursed Harry for eternity. "Now, if you will follow me, we will give you a tour of the grounds." He scanned the boys, noting their eyes and how some of them were willing. But the one he wanted first, or maybe the only one he wanted, was still red-faced and focusing on Harry.

Chapter 33: Where the Gachent and Pomm Play

"I don't think I can take another night of hearing Adeline and her whore husband." Doxy shuddered for the millionth time, the cries rising in his memory unbidden.

He and Fedvich were back in the carriage. The last house they looked at was horrid, the land worse. The only good thing about it was the fifteen-minute ride from the duke's castle.

"We have one more to peruse today, darling."

The man had a way of distracting him from the worst things as easily as snapping fingers. Doxy watched Fedvich flip over the paper in his hand. "It wasn't built that long ago."

"Are you sure we cannot go live in Gachent?"

"While I would normally jump at thc chance, you signed a contract." Fedvich folded up the piece of paper, tucking it away in his jacket pocket as he studied Doxy's face. "If it were only Regus in charge of these contracts, I would readily take you, but it is the king for whom you signed for. We just train and house you."

"I'm part of The Seven, that contract shouldn't matter. A privilege or something."

"Darling, the privilege of being part of The Seven is the hefty monthly allowance and the knowledge that you are equal with the six deadliest known." He stretched his legs out. "The contract holds for all, no matter if you are regular infantry, to one of us."

Doxy knew Fedvich was being reasonable, but it still irritated him. "I'm not deadly. At all. Why am I a member of The Seven?"

Fedvich canted his head. “If you had been recruited like me, saved and thrown into the middle of a battle the next day, you would be just as deadly as we are within a year.”

That had to be a lie. Doxy snorted, shaking his head at his lover. “Are you trying to get me hard so you can fuck me against the stables like the first one?”

“While that is a great idea, we would need to change it up. Perhaps the kitchen this time.” Fedvich said with a flash in his eyes, then he sobered. “I’m speaking the truth. You have the thing that makes us... us, and the other soldiers nameless. You just need a chance to shine. But I hope you don’t get that chance.” Fedvich turned away, his jaws tight. “I will not see you in a war.”

“When you talk like this, it’s like you’re ageless, like Slayth,” Doxy said, awestruck by his lover.

Fedvich made a face. “Never compare me to Bloodbath ever again.”

Doxy laughed. “Is it really that bad? It wasn’t in Gachent.”

“He’s nice to you.”

“What have you seen him do that makes you get all disgusted?” Doxy leaned forward a little, loving the travel time between places because it gave them a chance to talk over several things without interruption. Fedvich’s groan and his face going pale made him second-guess his question, but then his lover explained.

“He can use blood to kill. He takes it from one body and can shape it into these shards and stab people with it, only three though. Something about the blood makes it disappear after each death it causes.” He lifted a shoulder. “Or he can drown others with it, and the worst I’ve ever seen him do is dissolve.”

“Is that where there are no bodies left?”

“Yes.”

“He did that with the thieves in Gachent. I didn’t see the way he did it because he stayed behind a wall of blood.”

“Be thankful you didn’t see how it happened.” Fedvich studied something outside the window. He then turned back to Doxy. “You’re interested in things that Regus, Slayth, Charn,

Harry, and Bertran have done, but you never ask about me. Why is that?"

Doxy looked at anything within the confines of the carriage but Fedvich, as he tried to come up with an excuse. His heart leaped into his throat. Fedvich would think him pitiful if he knew the truth. He squeezed his eyes shut when he noticed his lover's brows raise. He was taking too long to lie. "I-I've asked the others."

"What?"

Doxy cracked open an eye. "I asked the others."

Fedvich slumped. "No, please tell me you didn't."

Doxy whimpered, knowing he'd disappointed him.

"They probably lied through their teeth!" Fedvich pinched the bridge of his nose. "Let me guess, Harry was the most forthcoming."

"No, actually, it was Regus." He looked behind him when Fedvich's eyes widened at him. Nothing was there, of course. "It's true."

"Regus?" Fedvich looked unsure. Gone was the polished sex god, and in his place was a man toying with his own fingers nervously. "What did he say? Give me the overall picture, if you will."

He wasn't sure if he liked this nervousness in his lover. "He said you were the most reliable of all of them. You learned everything on your own and surprised them every time they turned around with how quickly you overcame challenges and fears. He said that you were the kindest and would have made a great healer if you had the power, with how often you support others."

Fedvich stared at Doxy, blinking slowly as his nose reddened. He looked away, sniffing and blinking quickly. "Did he really say that?"

"He did."

He drew a deep breath and let it go while looking out the window. "I suppose Regus isn't so bad after all."

Doxy smiled, "No, he isn't." He then frowned. "Why is it that I'm the one getting him up in the morning and making sure he's dressed? You're least likely to get caught with your speed and you've known him the longest!"

Fedvich snorted, then chuckled. "My dear Doxy, it's the closest we could come to sending you into battle."

"Are you serious?!" When Fedvich nodded, he groaned. "I thought you were all joking. Do you know how many times my life has flashed before my eyes?"

His lover's grin was dark as he said, "It builds character." Then Fedvich glanced back out the carriage window. "Ah, we're here!"

Doxy shook his head, still amazed at how quickly Fedvich could bounce back to a neutral state of mind from extremes. He watched Fedvich reach for the door and open it before the carriage had fully stopped. He followed his lover, pausing on the step down. "We can't afford this! I do not get my inheritance until my parents die."

"Let's still explore, love." Fedvich smiled, studying the stone facade of the grand mansion.

After the housekeeper finished showing them every corner and closet two hours later, Doxy collapsed in the carriage, rubbing his weak knee. He didn't hear where Fedvich told the driver to go next. "That house is beyond us."

"We will see." Fedvich stated, sitting across from him. "You're tired. Sleep if you can, I will wake you when we get there."

Doxy wasn't sure when he drifted off, but he woke to Fedvich's lips on his. He murmured, trying to stretch out in the bed, but they weren't in bed. He blinked, focusing on the blue and yellow fabric of the interior of the hired carriage. "Town?" He asked, hearing all the noise outside before glancing out the window to watch a carriage and horse pass.

"Yes, we've come to buy that house."

Doxy blinked. "Which one?"

"The last one, the one you liked. I saw how your mouth dropped at every threshold."

Doxy's stomach filled with rocks and butterflies. "Fedvich, we cannot afford it. We couldn't."

"Hush, come on." Fedvich got out of the carriage and waited for Doxy to come out behind him before going up the few steps to the bank's door. There a man straightened from leaning against the wall. "Hello, Sir Bennett. Thank you for meeting me here after making that list of fine houses."

Doxy watched the two shake hands.

"Not at all, not at all! I hope you have found one to your liking?"

"Yes, let's go in and I shall purchase it straight away."

"Oh! Well, yes! Let's."

Doxy trailed behind the two men, as if he were dreaming still. It all seemed so unreal. They entered and walked directly into an office at the far end, where Fedvich met another man he called by name and shook his hand. What was his lover doing playing at this game?

"Which house was it?"

"The Sun's Grove."

"Splendid!" Bennett cried, fumbling through a case with papers before finding what he wanted and pulling the sheets out.

After the men passed the papers about a few times, signing here and there, Doxy found himself sweating profusely. He pulled at his collar, swearing it was hotter than summer in the room. He looked up when Fedvich said his name. "Yes?"

"Give us a moment, gentlemen, if you would." Fedvich smiled that charming smile, the two men blushed and tripped all over themselves to do Fedvich's bidding. His lover closed the door behind them, before crossing the room and quickly undoing the laces of Doxy's shirt and pulling the collar loose. "Don't pass out on me yet. I won't have anyone else laying hands on you, but I cannot carry you out by myself."

"You can't. This is too much. We will lose everything!"

Fedvich laughed. "Doxy." He placed his hands on his shoulders. "We are not poor."

"We're not that rich either!"

Fedvich chuckled, looking at the table and picking up a slip of paper. "Darling, see this number here?"

Doxy stared at it, blinked, and stared some more. There were too many numbers following behind the first. He looked up at the top of the statement, reading Fedvich's full name. He looked back down at the last line. "How... why...?"

Fedvich placed him in a chair. "Look at me. You have the answers to these questions already."

Doxy felt his head wobble. "Mercenary."

"And?"

"Tutelage of... oh..." Doxy stared. "You're going to have to teach me to teach sex."

"Not a chance. You're mine, and now the house is mine, and we have far too many rooms to fuck in before you pass out. Right?"

Doxy salivated, already picturing their sexcapades. "Yes, yes, my love, m-my sex god. Anything you wish."

Chapter 34: I Put a Spell on You, and Now You're Mine

He was old.

Fedvich wasn't too aged to learn, though. He'd just learned that Doxy wasn't out of his jealous stage. Better yet, he knew now that Doxy could become jealous. Damn Quin and his random visit and his incessant talking. There was a reason people paid him to have his mouth on them; Quin wouldn't shut up otherwise.

His love had him on his knees, again. Apparently, Addy and Viscountess Pomm weren't the only ones with a dominant streak. Doxy just didn't let his show until he was upset. His lungs and lips burned with the abuse, even his tonguc was a bit sore. Every bit of it was worth it to see Doxy wild and taking control. Gods fucking those eyes blazing nearly had him spilling alone.

With a rough tug to his hair, the hard dick popped out of his mouth. His lips were accosted by Doxy's, as his lover lifted him to his feet. Then that growling voice he'd only heard his love use on this day said, "Sit in my lap."

Fedvich panted, and quickly did as he was told. He spread his ass cheeks and bit his bottom lip as the wet head prodded his entrance. That dick slid into him and his breath caught. He was absolutely fascinated by Doxy's ass, but this side of his lover had him giddy and on the precipice in no time.

His hair was tugged again, and he arched back over Doxy's shoulder. A vice wrapped low around his hips. His breath was rammed out of him. He'd barely sucked one back in before he cried out at the next rough thrust.

"I'm. Not. Ready. For. Anyone. Else. To. Have. You. Dammit." Each word punctuated by a slapping thrust deep into Fedvich.

Was it a deterrent to his lifestyle? A little. Did he want Quin to come back over tomorrow so Doxy would fuck him hard again? Gods, yes. The stamina Doxy had while being jealous wasn't a concern. Not when it ended in several rounds of fucking like this. Like Doxy was marking him as his own and trying to make it permanent.

He thought buying a house for the man would be enough, but perhaps he should put a ring on it, too.

Fedvich hissed as teeth sank into his shoulder. Gods he was so fucked. Fucked in the head. Fucked because he liked a little bit of pain with his fucking. Fucked because he was desperately in love and loved by the man pounding so hard into him the chair was scooting across the floor and creaking like it was about to snap into splinters. And fucked because this man felt so good in him, on him, and around him that he couldn't think of anything else.

With two more hard thrusts, Doxy held him tight as he pumped his seed into him.

He was indeed old. Losing his touch. He'd cum too soon, too fast, and too many times to join his lover in his orgasm.

Doxy licked his bite. Fedvich slumped, finally able to breathe in enough to sate his burning lungs. He turned his head, nuzzling into Doxy's thick sweaty neck.

"Any more of your students coming by?"

"Mmm I hope so. If they do, are you going to fuck me like this again?" He chuckled as Doxy had the audacity to blush. "We still have six more rooms to consummate in."

"You have to teach me."

Fedvich groaned. "Dox, if I do that, I won't be hard long enough to bring you pleasure." He rose and fell with Doxy's huge sigh.

"Oh, I'm supposed to make sure you have enough water and food..."

"Don't you start!" He turned in Doxy's lap carefully, catching the cheesy little grin on his lover's face. "I'm old, but I can take care of myself."

"Are you sure, Father of Gachent?"

His heart swelled in his chest. So cheeky, so open now, and still able to blush and stammer. He pinched Doxy's cheeks before stealing a kiss. Then another. "I'll teach you a few things. Here and there. But you have a job to do. A Vicious to wake every morning, and a Father of Gachent to sate. Think you can handle all of that?"

Doxy's face darkened a shade. "For you, yes." Those lips then pouted as he whined, "Do I really still have to wake Regus?"

Sneak Peek at My Husband Wants to Keep Me Sated – Final Book

Chapter 1: Auntie, I Crave Violence

The carriage was stuffy. What made it worse was she couldn't open a window, or the dust from the road would pour in. Dust made everything worse.

"Where are we going?" She asked, knowing the answer she would get already. She peered at her 'auntie.' The woman was not blood related; she couldn't be. The woman that sat across from her with her 'uncle' was pale, slender, blonde haired, and a true proper lady of the times in her perfect dress and hairstyle. Her uncle was much the same in the pale and slender part.

Lilyanna had learned at a young age that none of the people that told her to call them a family member, were not family at all. She rotated between three 'aunties' and a 'mother' every other year. And every other year, her last name changed. Lily hadn't a clue as to who she was.

"You will know when we get there, dearest."

The nasally voice grated on her nerves. This was her least favorite 'aunt' by far. Too strict and too demanding.

Her only connection to her identity was a man who looked like her. Not as dark as her, but he had red hair and a devilish smile she learned to mimic when she was twelve. Her Uncle Harry was the best person she knew, other than her lifelong guard, Rix. He was loving, if not a bit overprotective, and a great listener. His penmanship wasn't like one would expect either. It was legible, and rather beautifully slanted.

She'd received a letter from him that very day. He told her to remain calm, and not tear apart the caregivers as well as the carriage. He knew she hated the carriage rides the most. He also said he would be waiting for her to arrive.

It made her hope that she was finally going to live with him. He led the life of a travelling wanderer with a band of men with similar talents. Uncle Harry was a tamer and enraptured crowds with his whip tricks. He also caught wild beasts that terrorized people, sometimes taming them, but other times he had to kill them. Hence all his scars.

Lily still didn't know why he had sharp metal things in his beautiful long hair. He always managed to change the subject. He did the same when she saw him leaving the first time. He had enough weapons on him to have one for fifty animals, she thought. Her uncle liked sneaking away at night after putting her to sleep with his stories.

It wasn't like his stories were boring, but somehow, she fell asleep anyway.

The carriage jolted to a stop, drawing her from her musings. She peeked out the window, and saw a lone building with horses in a fenced in field. "Are we really stopping for a break?"

Her auntie's lips pressed together. "Your uncle demanded we take a few extra stops to let you out and walk. For your health."

"He said our health dear. Perhaps he did mean, Lilyanna's health." Her 'uncle' pondered drolly.

Lily didn't care; she opened the door and bounded out. She ignored her aunt's demands on decorum and decency. With a good stretch she smiled and tilted her head back to let the sun warm her face. She watched a large bird circle overhead as her aunt and uncle clambered out of the carriage.

Her aunt promptly entered the building.

Then rushed out with a gasp. Lilyanna pretended to still be interested in the bird soaring as she watched the scene from the corner of her eye. Her uncle rushed to his wife's side in an instant.

"Why I never! There was a half... he was...! Good gods, look!"

Lilyanna and her uncle did. A man stood leaned against the wooden slats between the door and the dusty windows, while another hand his hands up on the door frame. Both had their shirts open and nasty looks on their faces.

She turned when she heard Rix's warning clicks. Whenever they clicked their tongue, she was to immediately go to his side. He stood behind the carriage, covered in their usual all black attire from head to toe, just out of sight of the men and her family.

The men leered at her auntie. The one leaning against the wall even went so far as to invade her space. He even sniffed her hair and shoved her uncle away.

"Aren't you going to do anything?"

"I'm hired to protect you, not them." Rix stated as if they were bored.

"Isn't it technically the same thing? They house me and all, you too." She put her hands on her hips and glared into the dark eyes hooded by their mask.

Rix glared right back at her. "You truly want me to go save those weak, ridiculous, greedy people?"

Lily had to think on that for a moment. She shook her head at herself. "Yes!" The men had already knocked her uncle down twice. The driver was yelling at them, but he had his hands full with the horses trying to run away.

Rix groaned, their body slumped as they dragged their feet toward the two brutes and her family that wasn't family. They turned to walk backward to warn her, "Remember. Don't watch." They waved her away with both clawed hands.

She watched them turn, arms out like a bird in flight and squeezed her eyes shut before she smelt the unmistakable metallic scent of blood. The sounds of flesh ripping made her shudder, but she didn't look.

Lily had made that mistake once and knew she would never do it again.

"Lilyanna!"

She cracked her eyelids open, then stared in disbelief. Rix was crouched over her auntie, blood dripping off them onto the once perfect dress. A clawed finger trailed sigils along her auntie's cheek. She never liked this side of them. The one that wanted to kill all of her family, except her Uncle Harry.

"Rix?"

They growled low, fingers clicking as he reached for the slender throat. Rix had her auntie trapped between them and the low wood porch of the building. A man still on his knees finally fell over onto his face. A stream of blood flowing from both bodies.

"Rix!"

They jerked their head up at her scream. Upon realizing she wasn't in danger, they slouched, hung their head, and sighed dramatically. "One day, I'll get to take a pound of flesh for every minute of torture you've put her through. And I'll take an ounce of blood from every coin you've stolen from Harry." The lithe form rose, stretching back. "I wonder what I will run out of first?"

"Rix, honey, please." Lilyanna fisted her hands at her sides to keep from trembling. Only to realize that she was still. She met the black eyes of her protector as they sauntered over and stood before her as it they hadn't killed two and threatened another.

"You called, *honey*?" Rix put their face too close to hers. "I told you to never call me that."

"I know. I love you. Do you still love me?"

Her guard laughed after relaxing again. "Of course I do. I love you with every fiber of my very being... honey."

Acknowledgements

I want to thank everyone who reads this, first and foremost. Without you, I wouldn't have the desire to keep writing. Thank you, and I hope you stay with these characters of mine whether you love them, hate them, or want to lick them.

Next, to my husband: you are the best. You know what you do... from the long conversations of me talking about these characters to you having to fix something I broke on the computer to just holding me while I doubt myself... I couldn't do this without you. I couldn't Life without you.

To my beta readers, fellow authors, and the Authortube community on YouTube: here we go again. Thank you! You're so supportive and awesome. I'm glad we found one another.

About the Author

Sam Wicker is a small-towner, married to a loving and the most supportive husband ever, and they have a furbaby named Kona. She's always wanted to write stories full of romance, real people doing fantastical things, and animals that awe. Sam hopes her stories inspire those suffering from anxiety and gives all her readers a place to escape to.

Her books are: Romantasy, Fantasy Romance, Romantic Comedy Fantasy, Dark Romantic Comedy Fantasy, Urban Fantasy, and very Adult - sexual content on page.

www.ingramcontent.com/pod-product-compliance
Lightning Source LLC
Chambersburg PA
CBHW051508050726
47594CB00010B/4017

* 9 7 8 1 9 6 5 7 7 0 1 0 8 *